Into the Ether

Zora Stone

Copyright © 2025 Zora Stone

All rights reserved.

No part of this publication may be copied, reproduced, distributed, or transmitted in any form or by any means—electronic, mechanical, photocopying, recording, or otherwise—without the prior written permission of the publisher, except in the case of brief quotations used in reviews or other noncommercial purposes permitted by copyright law.

This is a work of fiction. Names, characters, places, and events are either products of the author's imagination or used fictitiously. Any resemblance to actual persons, living or dead, or actual events is purely coincidental.

Print ISBN: 978-1-971405-05-6

Publisher: Smut by Design

www.zorastone.com

For the girl who broke first.
And still built something anyway.
Sometimes when you fall apart, everything falls into place.
And if not?
There's still holy-shit-we're-alive pancakes.

Previously in the Ether Chronicles

A quick refresher before we dive back into the mist

Hey there, lovely readers! Ready to step back into Bree's world? Here's what you need to remember from *Crown of the Mist* before we get to the good stuff:

Our girl Bree has been surviving on her own in a rundown apartment, carrying trauma from her abusive past—while mysterious silver mist keeps following her around. (Spoiler: it's not just pretty atmospheric effects.)

Her childhood friends—Rhett, Jace, Gray, Theo, and Wes—have been keeping protective watch from a distance. Because apparently, they're all secretly pining and terrible at communication. Classic.

Things got tense when her creepy landlord Phil turned out to be way more dangerous than your average slumlord. During a terrifying confrontation, Bree's power finally awakened—think ice, mist, and enough magical fury to launch a grown man across a room. Extremely satisfying.

The boys realized magic is real (*surprise!*), Bree realized she's not powerless (*double surprise!*), and they all ended up in an attic where a mysterious door revealed an impossible room... and a crown that called Bree "Queen of the Mist."

She touched it. Everything went white.

And here we are.

Oh—and someone's been watching from the shadows, pulling strings this whole time. But we'll get to that.

Welcome to *Into the Ether*.

Hope you're ready for awakening powers, ancient sanctuaries, and some very intense conversations about feelings.

(And yes, Thane is coming. You're welcome.)

Trigger Warnings

Thank you for reading *Into the Ether*. This book contains themes and content that may be triggering to some readers. Please review the following warnings before proceeding:

Emotional & Psychological Themes

- **Ongoing Trauma Recovery** – Bree continues processing childhood abuse and its lasting impact

- **PTSD & Trauma Responses** – Panic attacks, dissociation, hypervigilance, and touch sensitivity

- **Trust & Vulnerability** – Emotional intimacy, abandonment fears, and protective withdrawal

- **Body Image & Self-Worth** – Feelings of inadequacy, shame, and being "unlovable"

- **Memory Bleeding** – Magical sharing of traumatic memories between characters

Violence & Threats

- **Stalking & Surveillance** – Continued monitoring by antagonistic forces

- **Physical Confrontations** – Both magical and non-magical violence

- **Threats & Intimidation** – Verbal and physical coercion

- **Blood & Injury** – Vampire feeding, magical wounds, and healing magic

Sexual Content & Intimacy

- **Explicit Sexual Content** – Detailed, consensual scenes between adults

- **Vampire Feeding** – Blood drinking in both sexual and non-sexual contexts

- **Polyamorous Relationships** – Multiple romantic/sexual bonds among central characters

- **Consent & Power Dynamics** – Exploration of magical influence and emotional agency

Supernatural & Magical Themes

- **Magical Coercion** – Powers that influence thoughts, emotions, or physical response

- **Identity & Transformation** – Awakening and adapting to magical abilities

- **Political Manipulation** – Control and surveillance by magical governing bodies

Family & Betrayal

- **Parental Abuse** – Continued fallout from Bree's abusive father

- **Betrayal by Trusted Figures** – Allies who aren't what they seem

- **Chosen Family vs. Blood Family** – Themes of found family, loyalty, and emotional inheritance

This list is offered to help ensure a safe and supported reading experience. If any of these topics are distressing, please proceed with care and compassion for yourself.

Thank you for walking with Bree—

Zora Stone

CONTENTS

Chapter 1
BREE

The white light doesn't fade—it shatters.

One moment I'm suspended in starlight, the ancient voice still echoing through my bones. The next, I'm stumbling backward as reality crashes in like a tidal wave. Sound rushes back in a disorienting flood: my ragged breathing, the creak of old floorboards, Theo's sharp intake of breath somewhere to my left.

My knees buckle.

Strong hands catch me before I hit the floor—Rhett's warmth at my right shoulder, Gray's steady grip on my left arm. My body should flinch like it always does when I'm touched without warning... but it doesn't. Not this time. Maybe I'm in shock. Or maybe something in me is finally too tired to resist.

"Easy," Rhett murmurs, his voice low and careful. "We've got you."

They guide me backward until the edge of the bed meets my legs, and I sink down gratefully, my whole body trembling with the aftershocks of whatever just happened.

I try to focus on the feel of his hand on my shoulder, Gray's fingers still wrapped around my forearm like he's afraid I might disappear. But everything feels strange, like I'm seeing the world through someone else's eyes. The mist that usually follows me everywhere has retreated, curling close to my skin like it's hiding.

Rhett's voice is low and careful. "Are you okay?"

Jace follows a second later, his worry barely masked by sarcasm. "What the hell was that?"

I open my mouth to say I'm fine—the automatic response I've perfected over years of deflection. But the words stick in my throat, caught between truth and habit.

"I..." I swallow hard, my hands shaking as I press them flat against my thighs. "I'm not fine."

The admission hangs in the air between us, heavier than any lie would have been. Wes moves closer, his dark eyes scanning my face with that quiet intensity that sees too much. Theo hovers near the foot of the bed, his analytical mind already working through what just happened.

"The crown," I whisper, staring down at my palms like they should still be holding something precious. The shimmer has faded now, but I can still feel the warmth, like a brand pressed into memory. The heat lingers. Like it left something inside me instead.

"You touched the crown," Theo says quietly, his voice carrying careful precision. "Whatever it was—it responded to you. And then everything collapsed."

"We all saw it," Gray adds, his sharp gaze never leaving my face.

I look toward where the impossible room had opened, where ancient stones had pulsed with their own inner light. But there's nothing there now. Just the same attic walls, the same dusty air. Even the crystalline daisies that had been growing through the floor are gone, leaving no trace they ever existed.

"The room," I say, confusion threading through my voice. "The space beyond the door—it was huge. Ancient. Where did it go?"

"Same place as the crown, I'm guessing," Jace mutters, running a hand through his hair. "Which is exactly nowhere we can follow."

Wes moves to the door, his footsteps silent on the old floorboards. He pulls it open cautiously, and I hold my breath, half-expecting that silver light to spill out again. Instead, there's just darkness. The faint outline of storage boxes and a broken light bulb hanging from a frayed cord.

"It's just a closet now," he says, his quiet voice carrying an edge of something I can't identify. "No crown. No glow." He runs his fingers along the doorframe, searching. "The symbol's gone too."

They all exchange looks—the kind of silent communication they've perfected over years of friendship. I should feel relieved that the mysterious door has returned to normal, that whatever magic pulled us here has faded back to ordinary wood and dust.

Instead, I feel empty. Like something vital has been carved out of my chest.

"Did anyone else hear..." I start, then stop. My voice feels too small. "Never mind."

"Hear what?" Rhett's voice is gentle but insistent.

"A voice." I wrap my arms around myself, suddenly cold. "When I touched the crown. It called me..." I swallow hard. "It called me queen."

Silence. Five sets of eyes watching me with expressions I can't quite read.

"We didn't hear anything," Theo says carefully. "Just the surge of power. The light."

Of course they didn't. Because whatever spoke to me wasn't meant for them.

It should be terrifying. It should feel like a mistake.

But it doesn't.

It feels like something from before. Before fear, before scars, before I started bracing for impact every time someone touched me.

Like the version of me that existed before everything got broken.

"This can't be real," I whisper, barely able to hear myself over the pounding in my chest. "Stuff like that doesn't just... happen."

No one argues with me. No one tries to explain.

I wrap my arms tighter around myself. "But I feel different."

The words taste strange. Too big. Too true.

"I don't know how. Just..." I exhale slowly. "Like something cracked open inside me. Not broken—just... not closed anymore."

The mist stirs at my words, unfurling from where it's been hiding against my skin. It doesn't reach for the others like it usually does—it stays close, protective, like it's guarding me from something.

"Hey," Rhett says softly, his thumb brushing over my shoulder. "Whatever just happened, we'll figure it out. Together."

"Will we?" The question slips out before I can stop it, raw and uncertain. I grip the blanket beneath me, grounding myself with something real. "Because right now I feel like I'm coming apart at the seams, and I don't even understand what's holding me together anymore."

Gray's hand tightens slightly on my arm, grounding me in the warmth of his touch. "You're not coming apart," he says softly. "But whatever this is..."

Theo steps forward, his voice calm and certain. "We've got you."

He meets my eyes, steady and unflinching.

"We see you, Bree."

I close my eyes, trying to make sense of the storm of sensation and memory swirling through me. The memory of the crown's weight in my hands, the voice that called me queen, the way the mist responded to my touch like it was coming home. None of it should be possible. Yet all of it feels more real than anything I've ever experienced.

"I keep waiting for this to feel wrong," I admit, opening my eyes to find them all watching me with expressions of fierce protectiveness and something deeper. Something I don't have words for.
"What just happened, what I felt... it should scare me. But it doesn't. It feels..."

"Right," Wes says from his spot by the door. "It feels right."

I nod, surprised by how much his understanding means. "How is that possible? How can something this impossible feel so natural?"

"Maybe," Jace says, his usual sardonic tone gentler than normal, "because it's not impossible. Maybe it's just been waiting for you to be ready for it."

The mist pulses once, like a heartbeat, and for a moment I swear I can feel the crown's presence even though it's gone. Like an echo of power that will never fully fade.

I stare at my hands again, flexing my fingers like I could still close around its weight. But there's only absence. The crown's disappearance feels like a phantom limb—something I should be able to reach for but can't quite touch.

It was real. I know it was real. The weight of it, the warmth, the way it seemed to sing when I touched it.

But now it's gone, and something inside me isn't. Something that feels ancient and new all at once, like a door that's been unlocked but not yet opened.

And something tells me it's not done with us yet.

Chapter 2
THANE

I kneel before the scrying mirror in the ruins of what was once a Scarborne sanctuary, dust motes dancing in the pale light filtering through cracked stone. The chamber breathes with dormant magic, old power sleeping in the walls like a dying heartbeat.

I haven't touched the mirror yet. I don't need to.

The air changes—sharpening, thickening—like the room is holding its breath. The mirror, smooth and dark as polished obsidian, begins to hum. Just faintly. Just enough.

That's when the light hits.

It explodes through the surface like molten silver, so bright I have to shield my eyes. The mirror *screams*, and the stones in the walls begin to sing—high, aching, ancient.

I stagger backward, breath caught.

No.

It can't be.

But it is.

She's here.

The light fades, leaving me gasping in the sudden dark. I stumble, catch myself on a fallen pillar, heart pounding hard enough to echo in my ribs.

Slowly, I step forward again—toward the mirror. Toward the thing I didn't summon.

The surface is already dark. Cold. Dead again.

But the air still hums. And from the shattered edges of the obsidian frame, silver mist curls—threading up like smoke from a lightning strike. It brushes across my skin, and I flinch.

Ether.

Not ambient. Not wild. *Hers.*

It pulls against me like gravity, like instinct, like recognition carved into bone.

The pull isn't just magical. It's *cellular.* Like some part of me I thought long-dead just remembered how to want.

I hate how easy it would be to give in to it. To follow.

"Well. That was dramatic."

I don't turn at the voice—can't. I'm still too stunned to summon the composure I usually wear like armor.

Stellan steps from the shadows, his gray cloak dust-covered from the journey here. One of the few contacts I trust. One of the fewer still who knows what I've been watching for.

"She's crossing through the fold," I say, voice rough with awe and something like grief. "The five lights, the tethering, the surge—everything fits. She's finally coming home."

Stellan snorts. Actually *snorts.*

"It didn't come from the fold," he says, dragging a hand through his dust-coated hair. "You idiot."

I blink, thrown. "What?"

"The surge," he says, gesturing vaguely at the humming stones. "That wasn't transplanar. It originated in the mortal realm. That city you refuse to set foot in."

My breath catches. If she didn't cross over... then she was *already there.* Hidden. Suppressed. Forgotten.

And I missed her.

"That's not possible," I whisper.

"Apparently it is." He shrugs, but the edge in his voice is real now. "And if the Council felt it too—"

Pain flares beneath my ribs, sudden and searing.

A summons. Burned into my skin like a brand.

I exhale sharply, already burying the part of me that wants to react. Wants to *run.* I have to be composed. Controlled. Exactly what they expect.

Stellan sighs. "And here we go."

He steps back, his expression softening for just a breath.

"You know nothing about her," he says. "Remember that."

I don't answer.

And then the Council takes me

The magic pulls me sideways through space, twisting light and shadow into a corridor of sound. And then I'm there.

The Chamber of Five is already in session.

The thrones encircle a shallow basin of mirrored stone, carved into the floor like a scar. Each seat is sculpted from the material of its wielder's domain—Elemental, carved of molten rock and ice-cracked crystal. Shifter, a throne of twisted roots that pulse like veins. Seer, moonglass streaked with fractures of time. Mentalist, polished steel that reflects nothing.

So gaudy it's almost offensive. But of course the Mentalists would demand a seat that reflects nothing and still manages to scream importance.

My place, as always, is last in the circle. Set slightly back. Lower than the others. A block of matte black stone—unadorned, unpolished, utilitarian. It doesn't glow or hum or shimmer. It just absorbs.

Like we do.

I sit without ceremony. Let them see how little I care for the theatrics they cling to.

Valdris is pacing, flames hissing softly beneath her boots. She never sits unless she's about to burn something.

Nyx is draped sideways across her throne, all predator grace and performative boredom. She's watching me without blinking. Never a good sign.

Eris leans forward, her silver eyes blank with prophecy. She doesn't blink at all.

And Marcus, of course, is already staring at me like I've broken protocol just by existing.

"You're late," Valdris says, not even looking in my direction.

"I wasn't invited," I reply. "Just summoned."

Nyx's mouth quirks. "Still defensive, Feeder?"

"Still obsessed with me, Shifter?"

She smiles. Sharp and slow. She always does love it when I bite.

It's easier for her to pretend she's not circling when the others are in the room.

"Enough," Marcus says. He doesn't raise his voice. Doesn't need to. His tone cuts through everything like frost.

"The surge," Eris says, voice hollow, drifting. "It broke something. Time bent."

"No," Valdris snaps. "Not time. Power. It cracked open and screamed. That wasn't elemental. Not even close."

"It wasn't *any* of us," Nyx says, pushing upright. "That was Scarborne. Pure. Unfiltered. Like it used to be."

"So the line survived," Marcus says. "Despite our efforts."

"One," Eris confirms. "Mortal realm. Female. Hidden. Shielded."

"Protected by who?" Valdris demands.

"Others," Eris says. "Not bonded. But touched. Pulled toward her, even if they don't know why."

Her gaze sharpens—just slightly. "And some of them... they'd die for her already."

I keep my expression neutral.

But inside, something twists.

Of course they would. Whatever charm she's using, it's working. That's what Scarborne blood does. It pulls. Promises. Makes people believe they matter.

That kind of power isn't random. It's tactical.

I just have to get there before she decides how to use it.

"We should have eradicated the line more thoroughly," Marcus says. "Their ability to bond made them dangerous. It gave them influence they didn't earn. Power they didn't deserve."

"It made them unpredictable," I say. "But useful. In the right hands."

Nyx arches a brow. "Useful to you, you mean?"

I shrug. "She's untrained. Surrounded. Emotional. You send one of you, and it escalates. You send me—she doesn't see the blade until it's too late."

Valdris studies me. "You're volunteering to kill her, then?"

"If I have to," I say. "But I'd rather get her under control first. Alive's easier to manage. Dead is messier."

"And if she tries to bond with you?"

"She won't," I lie. "There's nothing in me worth taking."

Eris tilts her head. "Your thread intersects hers. Faint, but present."

"Coincidence," I say flatly.

"Convenient," Marcus murmurs. "Expendable."

I nod. "Exactly."

One by one, they vanish. Magic curling them back into their domains, into their power, into their ignorance.

I remain seated in the dark.

Not because I was dismissed.

But because I have decisions to make.

She's here. And they've just handed her to me.

If she's what they fear, I'll know first.

If she's worse—

I'll handle it.

They think they've sent a weapon.

What they don't know is that I never needed permission to strike.

Chapter 3
RHETT

Heat wakes me.

Not the good kind—the suffocating, crawling heat that makes you want to tear off your own skin. I surface from sleep gasping, my t-shirt soaked through with sweat that shouldn't exist. The room is cold. I can see my breath in the air, which means the radiator's busted again.

So why does it feel like I'm burning from the inside out?

I swing my legs over the side of the bed, bare feet hitting the floor. The shock of cold should help, but it doesn't. If anything, the contrast makes the heat worse—like my body's rejecting everything that isn't fire.

The bathroom mirror shows me what I already know. I look like hell. Dark circles, stubble, hair sticking up at angles that defy physics. But it's my eyes that stop me cold. They're bloodshot, sure, but there's something else. A flicker of gold in the hazel that wasn't there yesterday.

I lean closer, squinting. Just a trick of the light. Has to be.

The faucet handle is ice under my palm as I twist it, cold water rushing into the basin. I splash it on my face, gasping at the shock. Steam rises up from my skin where the water hits.

Steam.

I stare down at my hands, water dripping from my fingers. The droplets hiss where they slide off my skin, steam curling as if I'm the hot pan.

"What the hell," I breathe.

My reflection stares back, wide-eyed and spooked. The gold flicker is still there, brighter now. Like embers catching the wind.

This isn't happening. This can't be happening.

I've always run warm—genetics, maybe, or all those years working out, building muscle. But this... this is different. This feels like something living under my skin, clawing its way out.

I press my palms to the mirror. Steam blooms instantly, fogging the glass around my fingers. The heat doesn't hurt exactly, but it's relentless. Insistent. Like it's trying to tell me something I don't want to hear.

You're changing.

The thought slams into me, sudden and unwelcome. I can't change. I won't. I'm the steady one. The reliable one. The one who keeps everyone else safe when the world goes to hell.

I'm not supposed to be the thing they need protecting from.

But I can't stay in this room, pacing like something's about to explode.

The hallway is quiet when I step out, my bare feet silent on the old hardwood. Bree's still up in the attic. Still sleeping, hopefully. After what happened last night... she needs it.

I drift toward the kitchen on autopilot, muscle memory guiding me while my thoughts stay stuck upstairs. She looked so small in that bed. Pale. Hollowed out. Like whatever the crown took from her isn't coming back.

The kitchen feels safer. Familiar. I can make coffee, keep my hands busy, pretend everything's normal until this—whatever this is—goes away.

I reach for the coffee pot. The metal's room-temp when my hand hits it, but that doesn't last. The handle warms beneath my palm, faster than it should. Not scalding. Just wrong.

"Shit." I drop it, more reflex than pain, the pot clanging against the counter.

"Smooth, captain."

I spin around to find Jace leaning against the doorframe, his golden hair sticking up in sleep-mussed spikes. He's wearing yesterday's clothes, which means he probably didn't sleep any better than I did.

"Morning," I mutter, turning back to the coffee maker. Maybe if I ignore the heat issue, it'll go away.

"You okay?" Jace pushes off the wall, moving to lean against the counter beside me. "You look like you got hit by a truck."

"Feel like it too." I grab a coffee filter, trying to focus on the simple task. Paper crinkles under my fingers—and then the scent hits me.

Burnt. Faint, but sharp. Like scorched paper.

I freeze, staring down. The edges of the filter are curling in on themselves, browning like they've been too close to an open flame.

"Dude." Jace steps closer, squinting. "Are you—"

"It's fine." I toss the filter into the trash, fast. Too fast. Like that'll stop him from seeing what he already saw.

"That filter just tried to self-destruct."

"Old batch," I say, not looking at him. "Probably already half toasted."

"Uh-huh." Jace doesn't push, but the doubt is all over his face. "Want me to handle the coffee? I promise not to melt anything."

"I've got it."

Even though I don't. Not really

But my hands are shaking now, and when I reach for another filter, I can feel the heat building in my fingertips. The paper starts to curl before I even touch it.

"Rhett." Jace's voice has gone serious, the teasing edge completely gone. "What's going on?"

I freeze, staring down at my hands like they belong to someone else. The heat pulses under my skin, rhythmic and insistent. Like a heartbeat made of fire.

"I don't know." The admission thickens in my throat. "I woke up hot. Burning. And now everything I touch..."

I trail off, because if I say it, I have to admit I might be a threat. And I can't be that. Not to them

Jace steps closer, his bright blue eyes studying my face with an intensity that makes me want to look away. "Hot how? Like fever hot, or—"

"Like fire under my skin. Ever since Bree touched that crown hot."

Something flickers across Jace's face—recognition, maybe, or understanding. "You think it's connected?"

"Has to be." I lean against the counter, the cool marble doing nothing to ease the heat crawling up my arms. "She does something impossible, and suddenly I'm a walking furnace. Can't be coincidence."

"Maybe it's not a bad thing." Jace's voice is careful, like he's testing a theory. "Maybe it's just... I don't know. Something unlocking. Like what happened to her."

"Unlocking what?" The question comes out harsher than I mean it to, sharp with fear I can't quite hide. "Being dangerous? Hurting people?"

"Being different," Jace says. "Being something we don't understand yet."

"I don't want to be different." The words rip out of me, raw and honest. "I want to be safe. I want to keep her safe. And how the hell am I supposed to do that if I can't even touch a coffee filter without setting it on fire?"

Jace opens his mouth to respond, but footsteps on the stairs cut him off. Light, familiar steps that make my chest tighten with equal parts relief and terror.

Bree appears in the doorway, hair mussed from sleep, one of my hoodies swallowing her small frame. She looks fragile in the morning light, still recovering from whatever happened to her last night. Still vulnerable.

"Morning," she says, voice soft and rough with sleep. Her eyes find mine across the kitchen, and she smiles—small but real. "Coffee smells good."

I haven't made any. Just burnt paper and whatever the hell is happening to me.

But I don't correct her. Can't. Because she's moving toward me with that unconscious trust she's finally started to show, and all I can think about is the heat radiating from my skin.

She slides up beside me, close enough that I can smell the vanilla scent of her shampoo. Close enough that she'll feel the heat rolling off me in waves.

"You okay?" she asks, looking up at me with those green eyes that see too much. "You look—"

"Fine," I cut her off, stepping back before she can touch me. "Just tired."

The hurt that flickers across her face is like a knife to the chest. She was reaching for me—something she never would have done a week ago—and I just pulled away like her touch would burn.

Which it might. Or I might burn her.

"Okay," she says quietly, wrapping her arms around herself. "I'll just... get some water."

She moves to the sink, and I watch her go, hating myself for the distance I've just put between us. Hating the thing inside me that's making me dangerous.

Jace catches my eye, his expression a mix of sympathy and concern. He knows. He sees exactly what's happening and why I can't let her close.

The problem is, pulling away from Bree might be the one thing that kills me.

But letting her close might be the thing that kills her.

I don't know what's happening to me. But I know one thing for certain—I can't let this thing inside me hurt the people I love.

Even if it means staying away from them forever.

Chapter 4
GRAY

The nightmare hits like ice water in my veins.

I'm small again—so small my feet don't touch the floor when I sit on the bed. My hands shake as I clutch something soft and worn, its fur matted from too many tears. The air tastes like burnt toast and cigarettes, acrid and wrong, making my stomach twist.

"You're just going to leave?!" The voice explodes through thin walls, making me flinch. "After everything I've done for you?"

I know that voice. Kevin. Bree's father. But I shouldn't be hearing it like this—shouldn't be *here* like this.

"I can't do this anymore, Kevin." The woman's voice wavers between sharp and broken, and something in my chest cracks at the sound. "I've tried. God, I've tried. But I'm done."

Claire. Bree's mother.

I press my hands over my ears, but the voices seep through anyway, poison through cracks. My heart pounds against my ribs as I squeeze my eyes shut, colors bursting behind my lids.

"You're not thinking about Bree." Kevin's voice turns mean—the way it always did right before something broke. "What kind of mother just walks out on her kid?"

"Everything I do is for her!" Claire's voice cracks like glass. "You don't understand. You never did."

I pull the bear tighter, clutching it to my chest. My fingers curl into its fur—so tight I feel threads pop.

She wouldn't leave me. She wouldn't.

Wait.

She wouldn't leave me?

The front door slams, shaking the walls. Everything goes quiet.

"Mom?"

The word slips from *my* lips.

But it's not mine.

It's hers.

Small. Trembling. So full of hope it hurts.

"Mommy?"

I slide off the bed, my socks silent on worn carpet. The hallway light cuts across the room, just enough to see the tear in the bear's ear. I fixate on it, blinking hard against the sting in my eyes.

Kevin's voice explodes again. "Damn it, Claire!" Something crashes, and I jump. "You're gonna regret this!"

I run to the window, pressing my hands against cold glass. Below, a figure cuts through the darkness, moving so fast she's almost running. Long dark hair streams behind her like a flag of surrender.

"Mom!" I bang on the window, but she doesn't look back. "Mom, please!"

She reaches the corner where the streetlight flickers—that broken one that never works right.

For a second, she pauses.

And I think—I hope—she's going to turn around.

But then...

A faint glow halos her figure. Soft, almost like moonlight. Just for a breath.

I blink.

And she steps into the shadows.

The night swallows her whole.

One moment she's there, and the next... nothing.

I shrink back from the window, clutching the bear to my chest, and slide to the floor. My knees hit the carpet as the first sob breaks free—

I wake up gasping.

My chest heaves like I've been drowning, cold sweat making my shirt stick to my skin. The room is too quiet, too dark, and for a moment I can't remember where I am. The taste of cigarettes lingers in my mouth, and I swear I can still smell burnt toast.

I sit up slowly, running a hand through my hair. My fingers shake.

What the hell was that?

The nightmare clings to me like smoke, every detail sharp and vivid. The texture of the bear's fur. The exact words of the fight. The way the light flickered around Claire before she disappeared.

I swing my legs over the side of the bed, my bare feet hitting the cold floor. The mist hovers at the edges of the room, thicker than usual, watching. Waiting.

I know that night.

Bree told us her mom left when she was little. But she never told us how. Never described the fight, or watching from the window, or...

The bear.

She never mentioned a bear.

My chest tightens.

It wasn't just a dream.

It felt like a memory.

And I don't know how that's possible.

My stomach drops as the implications hit me. I shouldn't know about the bear. I shouldn't know the exact words Kevin and Claire said to each other. I shouldn't know what it felt like to be six years old, clutching a stuffed animal while your world falls apart.

But I do.

I remember the night it happened—hearing something through our shared wall. Shouting. A door slamming. I was probably eight or nine, and I looked out my own window when I heard the commotion. I saw someone walking away under the streetlight, but I didn't think much of it at the time.

I never told Bree I saw her mother leave.

And she never told me she watched it happen.

So how do I know?

The mist swirls closer, and I feel something tug at my chest—like a thread pulling tight. The sensation is foreign but familiar, like déjà vu made physical.

I need air. I need space. I need to think.

The kitchen is dark when I walk downstairs, but I'm not surprised to find I'm not alone. Rhett leans against the counter, his broad frame silhouetted in the faint light from the window. He doesn't look surprised to see me either.

We stare at each other for a long moment.

"You felt it too," he says quietly. It's not a question.

I don't answer right away. Can't. Because admitting it makes it real, and I'm not ready for this to be real.

"It wasn't a dream," I say finally.

"No." Rhett's voice is rough, like he's been awake for hours. "I don't think it was."

Footsteps on the stairs draw our attention. Wes appears in the doorway, his dark hair sticking up at odd angles, eyes bloodshot. He doesn't speak, just goes straight to the cabinet and pulls out a box of cereal. Starts eating it dry, straight from the box.

None of us comment on how his hands shake slightly.

"The bear," I say, testing the words. "She had a stuffed bear. Brown, with a torn ear."

Rhett nods slowly. "She called it Bear. Real creative, our Bree."

"She used to bring it to sleepovers," Wes adds, his voice quiet. "Until she got too old and started leaving it at home."

We all knew about the bear.

But we shouldn't know how it felt in our hands that night.

Shouldn't know the comfort of pressing our face into its worn fur—while our world shattered around us

"This is impossible," I whisper.

"Yeah," Rhett agrees. "But here we are."

The mist drifts between us, silent and knowing. And I wonder what any of this means now. I think about Bree upstairs, probably asleep in that big bed we built for her. Does she know what's happening? Can she feel us the way we felt her?

"What happened when she touched that crown?" Wes asks, echoing my thoughts.

"I don't know." I lean against the wall, trying to process the implications. "But something bled through. Her memory became... ours."

"Just hers?" Rhett's voice carries an edge of something I can't identify. "Or all of them?"

The thought sends a chill down my spine. Bree has decades of memories I've never seen. Trauma I've only glimpsed the edges of. If they start bleeding through like this one did...

"We need to tell her," Wes says.

"Tell her what?" I shake my head. "That we're suddenly experiencing her childhood trauma? That we felt her terror and abandonment like it was our own?" I run a hand through my hair. "She'll think we're insane."

"We might be," Rhett mutters.

But we're not. I know we're not. The memory was too vivid, too specific, too real. I can still taste the fear in my mouth, still feel the way my hands... No. Her small hands trembled as she clutched that bear.

The worst part isn't the impossibility of it.

The worst part is knowing she's been carrying that night—that level of pain and abandonment—alone all these years. While I lived right next door, hearing sounds through the wall but never saying anything because I was too afraid. I didn't know what true fear was.

"She was so small," I whisper.

"She's still small," Wes says, his voice rough with something that might be guilt. "Still carrying all of it."

We fall into silence again, each lost in our own thoughts. The mist continues to drift between us, and I wonder what all of this really means.

The sky outside the window is starting to lighten, painting everything in shades of gray.

Soon Bree will wake up, and we'll have to pretend.

Pretend we don't know things no one else should.

We'll have to act normal while carrying pieces of her past in our chests like shrapnel.

I think about the way she looked at us yesterday—confused, vulnerable. Finally trusting us with something that she would insist on handling herself. Letting us help her make sense of what happened. How can we do that when we don't understand it ourselves?

"What if this is just the beginning?" I ask, the words slipping out before I can stop them.

Neither of them answers. Because we're all thinking the same thing.

If one memory can bleed through this easily, what else is waiting in the dark corners of her mind?

And what happens when she realizes we're not just protecting her anymore—we understand, because we've lived it too.

The mist pulses once, like a heartbeat, and I know with bone-deep certainty that everything changed the moment she touched that crown. Not just for her.

For all of us.

Chapter 5
BREE

Sleep used to be my escape. Now it feels like hiding.

I've been doing too much of both lately—three days since the crown, maybe four. Time blurs when you spend most of it unconscious, trying to outrun the weight pressing against your chest every time you're awake.

The room is too quiet when I finally surface, late morning light filtering through curtains I don't remember closing. No voices drifting up from downstairs like there used to be. No laughter echoing through the halls, no easy banter that made this place feel alive.

At the foot of the bed, someone's left a hoodie. Folded carefully, like an offering. I can't tell whose—they all smell like cedar and safety and things I'm afraid to want too much.

I pull it on anyway, drowning in fabric that makes me feel smaller than I already am.

The mist stirs faintly when I swing my legs off the bed, curling around my ankles like it's checking to make sure I'm real. It used to feel like it was following me around, showing up when I was upset, hurt, or angry. Now? Now it never leaves. My constant companion since everything changed.

Since everything broke.

Because of me.

I clench my fists as I head to the hallway, willing it away, but it just curls closer. Like it knows I need it, even when I don't want it there.

The kitchen hums with activity when I finally make it downstairs, but the energy feels wrong. Muted. Like someone turned the volume down on the house itself.

Jace leans against the counter, coffee mug cradled in his hands. His golden hair catches the morning light, but his usual grin is nowhere to be found. Just polite acknowledgment when our eyes meet.

Rhett stands at the sink, shoulders tense as he scrubs a pan that's probably already clean. He doesn't look up when I enter, and something in my chest tightens at the careful distance he's maintaining.

Wes sits at the table, hoodie pulled up despite the warmth, staring down at his bowl like it holds answers to questions he won't ask. His usual quiet feels different now. Heavier.

Theo thumbs through a book nearby, but I can tell he's listening to everything, cataloging the tension like he always does when he's trying to solve a problem none of us understand.

The toaster pops, sending up a thin curl of smoke. Someone burned the bread.

"Well," I say, aiming for lightness, "at least I'm not the only one having kitchen disasters anymore."

Jace's mouth quirks up—barely—but the others don't react. The joke falls flat, landing in the silence like a stone dropped in still water.

I glance at Rhett, concern overriding my own discomfort. "What happened?"

"Nothing." The word comes out too fast, too flat. A practiced lie that doesn't even try to be convincing.

My stomach drops. Since when does Rhett lie to me? Since when does any of this feel so... careful?

I move to sit across from Wes, hoping proximity might break through whatever wall has gone up between us. "Morning," I try, keeping my voice soft.

He mumbles something that might be a greeting, still not meeting my eyes. His fingers drum against the table, restless in a way that's not like him.

"Wes?" I lean forward slightly. "Are you okay?"

That gets a reaction. He looks up sharply, and for a split second, I see something that makes my breath catch.

A soft, pulsing glow at the base of his throat. Like light moving beneath his skin—not bright, but unmistakably wrong. Unnatural.

I blink, and it's gone.

Or maybe it was never there.

But the way Wes freezes tells me otherwise. He caught me staring, caught the recognition in my eyes.

"It's nothing," he mutters, standing abruptly to clear his bowl.

That's the second lie in five minutes. The mist stirs around my feet, responding to the spike of anxiety in my chest.

They're all lying. Not to be cruel—I know them well enough to recognize protection when I see it. But they're protecting me from something. Or protecting themselves from me.

"How are you doing?" Theo's quiet question cuts through my spiraling thoughts. It's the first time anyone's asked me directly since... since everything changed.

The automatic response rises to my lips like it always does. The careful deflection I've perfected over years of deflecting concern.

"I'm fine."

The words barely leave my mouth before heat pulses through my chest—low and coiling, like someone tightening a string beneath my ribs.

At first, I think I'm imagining it.

A faint light, bleeding through the fabric of my sleeves. Soft. Gold-white. Wrong.

I push the hoodie sleeve up with shaking hands, needing to see—

And there it is.

Gold-white light tracing every raised line on my arm. Gentle, but unmistakable.

The old wounds from childhood. The newer ones from Jason.

All of them lit from within, like my body's trying to confess something I haven't admitted yet.

The guys all see it.

Jace curses under his breath, coffee mug frozen halfway to his lips.

Rhett moves like he's going to come closer, then stops—hands clenched, jaw tight.

Wes goes rigid, the faint glow at his throat flickering like a candle in wind.

Theo watches with something that might be awe, but doesn't flinch.

Heat blooms beneath my skin, and I can't stop it—can't make it retreat.

Not now. Not with all of them watching.

Shame rises, sharp and immediate. Not because they know I'm lying.

Because this is happening at all. Because something inside me is still causing things I can't explain. Still glowing in ways I can't control.

I wrap my arms around myself, trying to make the light smaller. Trying to make myself smaller.

"I was trying to protect you," I whisper.

I think of Wes—of the flicker at his throat, the way he froze.

The way Rhett won't look at me.

The way Jace hasn't made a joke in days.

They haven't said anything. Not about the crown. Not about me. Not about whatever this is.

But something's happening. Something more than just me.

"You're all acting different." The words come out quiet, devastated. "You're pulling away, and I don't even know what I am anymore."

I look at each of them—these men who've stood between me and everything I've been afraid of, even when I didn't want them to. And now? Now I feel like they're slowly drifting out of reach.

"I see it. I see how you look at me now. Like I'm something you have to manage. Like I'm too much again." My voice cracks on the last word. "Like I'm dangerous."

The truth sits between us, sharp and painful.

"If I broke something inside you," I continue, staring down at my still-glowing scars, "if touching that crown did something to all of us—I didn't mean to. I didn't want to hurt anyone."

The silence stretches too long. Heavy with everything none of us know how to say.

I push back from the table, the chair scraping against the floor. The sound cuts through the quiet like a blade.

"I need some air."

I don't wait for a response. Can't. Because if I stay here one more second, wrapped in their silence and half-truths, I'll shatter.

The mist follows as I head for the door, curling around my legs like it's trying to slow me down. But I keep moving, past their watchful eyes, past the weight of everything I can't fix.

Behind me, I hear movement—someone standing, maybe reaching out. But no one follows.

No one stops me.

And maybe that tells me everything I need to know.

Chapter 6
THEO

She left. Just walked out. Final in a way none of us want to name.

No one moves.

Rhett is frozen by the sink again, white-knuckling the edge of the counter like it's the only thing keeping him upright. Jace has both hands tangled in his hair, pacing without direction. Wes hasn't looked up from the spot where Bree used to be.

I set my mug down. The sound feels too loud in a room that just lost its center. I want to say something, but I don't. Words are supposed to be my thing—the calm voice in the middle of the storm. But right now, I've got nothing.

"That was bad," Jace says, voice rough. "Like. Bad-bad."

"She glowed." Wes's voice is flat.

"Yeah," Jace mutters. "So did you."

That gets Wes's attention. His head snaps up, eyes sharp. "It's not the same."

"Looks the same from here."

"It's not."

Rhett turns around slowly. His face is pale. Jaw clenched tight.

"She thinks she's dangerous."

"She thinks she did this to us," I say quietly.

Jace lets out a bitter breath. "I mean. Maybe she did."

"Don't." Rhett's voice cuts like a blade. "Don't even say that."

"I didn't mean—"

"Yes, you did."

The silence stretches. Not empty this time—jagged. Heavy. Honest.

Footsteps. A pause in the hallway.

Gray rounds the corner, hoodie half-zipped, hair still damp from a shower. He slows when he sees us, reads the air in half a second.

"What... what happened?" His eyes flick toward the front door.

Wes doesn't move. Jace glances away.

"Fuck," Rhett mutters, barely more than a breath.

Gray's voice hardens. "She looked like she was about to cry."

Rhett slams a hand against the counter. Not hard. But loud enough.

Gray steps into the room, jaw tight. "What the hell did you all do?"

"We fucked up," Rhett says, turning to face us. "We let her think she's the problem. Again."

Gray's expression shifts. "What problem? What's going on?"

Rhett runs a hand through his hair, the weight in his eyes heavy. "The crown. She touched it, and everything changed. Her. Me. Wes." He looks down at his hands. "I don't even know what's happening to me, but I can't stop it."

"And instead of talking to her about it," I say, "we just—what? Pretend she won't notice?"

"She already noticed," Jace mutters. "She just didn't know how to say it."

Wes finally moves. Slowly. Hands clenched. Shoulders tight.

"I don't know what's going on right now." His voice is rougher than I've ever heard it. "But I know I'm not okay."

Jace swears under his breath.

Wes doesn't stop. "I keep seeing her. Dreams. Memories that aren't mine."

Gray watches him closely. Quiet. Calculating.

No one speaks.

So I do. "You think you're connected to her."

Wes nods, slow. "I think I was always waiting for her. And now that she's here, it's like I can't stop wanting to feel what she feels."

Jace finally sits. Hard. Like his legs gave up.

"She's out there thinking she ruined us," he says. "And we're in here acting like she's the threat."

"She's not the threat," Rhett says. "She's the reason we're still standing."

I glance toward the hallway. At the soft curl of mist still lingering there.

"We have to tell her."

Jace looks up. "Tell her what? That we're all glowing and cracking and seeing things?"

"That we're changing," I say. "And it's not her fault."

Gray exhales through his nose, sharp. "Did anyone think to tell her that? He crosses his arms when no one answers. "Then we'd better figure out what this is. Fast."

The silence that follows feels different. Not the brittle quiet of secrets and denial, but something heavier. The weight of truth we're finally ready to carry.

I've always been good at reading people—seeing the patterns, the connections others miss. It's why I notice when Jace stops deflecting with humor. Why I catch the way Wes's hands shake when he's not looking.

Why I can tell that Gray's anger isn't really at us—it's at himself for not being here when Bree needed him.

But this feels bigger than individual patterns. Bigger than just the five of us trying to figure out our own changes.

The mist still lingers in the hallway, faint but persistent. Like it's waiting for something. Like it knows we're not done yet.

I think about Bree's face when her scars lit up—not just shame, but recognition. Like some part of her had been expecting this. Like she's been carrying the weight of what we're becoming long before any of us understood what was happening.

"She's been protecting us," I say quietly. "From the beginning. Even when she didn't know what she was protecting us from."

Rhett looks up. "What do you mean?"

"Think about it. She's been pulling away, trying to keep distance between us and whatever she thought she might do to us. But we've been doing the same thing to her." I meet each of their eyes in turn. "We've been so afraid of what we're becoming that we forgot the most important thing."

"Which is?" Gray asks.

"That she's been becoming something too. And she's been doing it alone."

The truth of it settles over us like the mist—quiet, inescapable, undeniable.

We can figure out the magic later. The glowing, the dreams, the hunger—all of it can wait.

But Bree can't.

Not anymore.

Chapter 7
JACE

Three a.m. tastes like burnt coffee and unspoken truths. I'm already on my second pot when footsteps creak down the hallway. Not surprised—none of us have been sleeping much since Bree started avoiding us. The house feels wrong with her hiding upstairs, like we're all walking on eggshells, waiting for something that might never come.

Wes appears in the doorway, moving with that careful quiet he's perfected over the years. He slides into his usual spot at the table without a word—same chair he's claimed since we moved in here. But something's different tonight. He looks like hell, dark circles under his eyes, hair a mess. But there's something else too. Something I can't quite put my finger on.

His face looks... sharper somehow. More defined. Like someone adjusted the contrast on a photo.

"Coffee?" I ask, already reaching for another mug.

He nods, not looking up from where his hands are folded on the table. I pour, add the ridiculous amount of sugar he pretends he doesn't want, and slide it across to him.

"Rough night?"

Another nod. The kind that says *you have no idea*.

I settle across from him, cradling my own mug like it might contain answers instead of caffeine. The silence stretches, but it's not uncomfortable.

Wes has always been quiet—it's one of the things I've always liked about him. No need to fill every moment with noise.

But this quiet feels different. Heavier.

"Rhett nearly set the kitchen on fire a few days ago," I say, testing the waters. "Not on purpose. Just... couldn't touch anything without it heating up."

Wes's eyes flick to mine. Dark, confused. "What do you mean?"

"Coffee filters. They started browning before he even touched them. And when he grabbed the pot..." I shake my head. "Steam rising off his skin like he was a damn radiator."

Wes goes very still. "That's not normal."

"No shit." I take a sip of coffee, grimacing at the bitter burn. "The man looked terrified of his own hands. Can't blame him."

"Is he okay?"

"Physically? Yeah. Mentally?" I shrug. "About as okay as any of us right now."

Wes is quiet for a long moment, staring down into his coffee like it might show him something. When he finally speaks, his voice is barely above a whisper.

"Gray had a dream the other night. One of hers, I think."

I set my mug down carefully. "How do you know?"

"He said it felt like... I don't know. Like he was inside her skin. Woke up shaking, said Claire's name like it was his mom's.

Something cold slides down my spine. "He just told you that?"

"Didn't have to. I could see it in his face. The way he looked at me like he'd just lived through something that wasn't his to live through." Wes meets my eyes, and there's something raw there. Vulnerable. *"It hit him hard."*

I don't question it. Should, maybe. A week ago I would have. But we're past the point of disbelief now. Past the point where any of this makes sense in normal terms.

"It's not just her, is it," I say.

"No."

"It's all of us."

We both look up.

Theo's in the doorway now, hair rumpled, eyes shadowed with the same exhaustion we've all been wearing.

None of us heard him approach. But it fits. Theo's always been the quiet one—watching, listening, waiting for the moment to speak.

He walks to the counter, grabs a mug, but doesn't pour anything. Just stands there, turning it in his hands like it might help him think.

"I've been having dreams too," he says quietly. "Not hers. Or maybe... not just hers."

He doesn't elaborate. Doesn't describe what he's seeing. But there's something in his voice—a weight that makes my chest tighten.

"They don't feel like memories," he continues. "They feel like warnings."

Something cold slides down my spine. "Warnings about what?"

"I don't know." Theo's grip tightens on the empty mug. "But whatever's coming... it's bigger than just us."

The air in the kitchen shifts—subtle, but I feel it. Like the pressure dropping before a storm. And for a second, just a breath, I swear I feel something respond to the spike of anxiety in my chest.

A fork on the counter lifts slightly, hovers for a heartbeat, then clicks back down.

We all stare at it.

Nobody says anything.

Theo glances at me, but doesn't comment. Doesn't ask. Just sets his mug down carefully and takes a step back.

Shit.

I clench my hands into fists and try to shake it off. But the air still feels wrong.

This isn't just Bree anymore. It's not just her scars lighting up or strange crowns appearing. Something's happening to us too.

Footsteps on the stairs save me from spiraling further. Heavy, familiar treads that could only belong to Rhett and Gray. They appear together, both in sweatpants and hoodies, both carrying the same weight of sleeplessness the rest of us wear like a second skin.

"Couldn't sleep," Gray says to no one in particular, moving to lean against the counter.

"None of us can," Theo replies without looking up.

They don't need explanation. Don't ask why we're all awake at three in the morning, sitting in a kitchen that feels too quiet without Bree's easy presence. They just join the circle, settling into the familiar rhythm of shared insomnia.

Rhett takes the chair next to Wes, careful not to touch the wood with his bare hands. Gray claims his usual spot by the window. And suddenly we're all here—all except the one person who should be.

The mist drifts through the hallway as if summoned by the thought, curling toward the center of our group like it's trying to fill the empty space she's creating between us. None of us mention it. We don't need to.

I glance around the room—at these four men who've been my brothers, my anchors, my family for longer than I can remember. We've always known how to carry each other through the hard times. How to exist together in the spaces between words.

This? We'll get through this too. Probably.

Chapter 8
WES

The smell of burnt toast hits like a punch to the gut.

Normally I'd make some crack about Jace's cooking skills. Today it just makes my stomach twist—not with nausea, but with something deeper. Hungrier. Like my body's been hollowed out and filled with static.

I'm hunched over the kitchen table, hands wrapped around a mug of coffee that's gone cold while I wasn't paying attention. The morning light streaming through the windows feels too bright, too sharp. Everything does. Sounds are louder, colors more saturated, like someone cranked all my senses up to eleven and forgot to give me the manual.

"Seriously?" Jace mutters, waving smoke away from the toaster. "This thing hates me."

Theo glances up from his book, lips twitching. "Or you just don't understand the concept of moderation."

"Moderation is for quitters."

Their banter should be comforting. Familiar. Instead it scrapes against my nerves like sandpaper. I press my palms flat against the table, trying to ground myself in something real.

That's when I notice Gray watching me.

Not glancing. *Watching.* His storm-gray eyes track my movements with an intensity that makes my skin prickle. There's something in his expression I can't place—confusion mixed with something else. Something that looks almost like hunger.

"You good?" Theo asks, following Gray's stare.

I shrug, not trusting my voice. Because I'm not good. Haven't been since the crown, since everything changed. Sleep comes in fragments now, broken by dreams that feel more like memories bleeding through from somewhere else. And this gnawing emptiness in my chest that food doesn't touch, rest doesn't ease.

"Yeah. Fine."

The lie tastes bitter.

Gray's jaw flexes, but he doesn't look away. If anything, his attention sharpens. Like he's trying to solve a puzzle I don't know I'm presenting.

I push back from the table, needing space, needing air. The fridge hums as I pull it open, cool air washing over my overheated skin. I'm not even hungry—not for food, anyway. But the emptiness claws at me, demanding *something*.

I grab the first thing I see. Cold chicken from last night. Take a bite standing there with the fridge door open.

The first taste is everything. Relief floods through me, warm and immediate. But it's not enough. It's never enough anymore.

A spoonful of leftover pasta. Better. A chunk of cheese. Bread with nothing on it. An apple, juice running down my chin.

The third bite doesn't even taste like food anymore. Just relief. Just the hollow ache finally, finally easing.

"Fuck," I breathe, head falling back as the tension I've been carrying for days starts to unravel.

The sound that slips out is involuntary—not sexual, but intense. Raw. Like I've been holding my breath for weeks and finally remembered how to exhale.

That's when I realize the kitchen has gone silent.

I turn around, apple juice still sticky on my chin, to find four sets of eyes staring at me. Jace is frozen with toast halfway to his mouth. Rhett's stopped mid-step, coffee mug suspended in air. Theo's book lies forgotten on the table.

And Gray... Gray's watching me like he's seeing something he recognizes but can't name. His pupils are dilated, lips slightly parted. There's a flush creeping up his neck that has nothing to do with embarrassment.

I close the fridge door like that'll somehow make this less mortifying. It doesn't.

"When did this start?" Theo's voice cuts through the silence, gentle but precise.

My hands clench at my sides. "It's not what you think."

"Then what is it?"

"I..." My throat works around words that won't come. "I don't know. But it's getting worse."

Theo's frown deepens, his gaze dropping to my chest. Following it, I catch a glimpse of myself in the microwave's reflection—and freeze.

There's light beneath my skin. Faint but unmistakable, tracing lines along my collarbone, my solar plexus. Right where Bree touched me after the crown.

I press my hand over it, trying to hide what's already been seen. But it's too late. They've all noticed now.

Shame floods through me, hot and immediate. Not just the hunger—though that's bad enough—but what it means. That I'm different. That I don't know what's happening to my own body. That Bree might see me like this.

I don't want her to see me like this. Not when I don't even know what I am.

I take a step toward the hallway, every instinct screaming at me to run. To hide. To pretend this isn't happening.

"Don't." Gray's voice stops me cold. Not commanding, just... certain.

I freeze, one foot already in the doorway.

"You're not the only one," Rhett adds quietly, lifting his hands. In the morning light, I can see the faint shimmer of heat rising from his palms.

The shame doesn't disappear. But it shifts, becomes something I might be able to carry instead of drown in.

"We don't tell her yet," Theo says, and there's steel beneath the gentleness. "Not until we understand what this is."

Rhett nods. "She's got enough to deal with."

"Unless it gets worse," Jace adds, his usual humor carefully restrained. "Then we make a grocery list."

The joke falls flat, but the intent behind it—the refusal to treat me like something broken—hits harder than any grand gesture could.

I sink back into my chair, hands still trembling. The cold ache in my chest hasn't disappeared entirely, but it's manageable now. Contained.

Gray is still watching me, but the intensity has shifted. Less confusion, more... recognition. Like he's seeing something that makes sense in a way it shouldn't.

Theo catches it too, his analytical gaze flicking between us with that quiet focus that misses nothing.

I don't sit right away. My hands are still shaking. My chest's still tight. That cold, empty ache still gnaws at the edges of everything.

But no one tells me to stop. No one pulls away.

They just... wait. Make room. And somehow that's worse and better all at once.

The hunger doesn't fade.

But it doesn't feel like a curse anymore.

It feels like something I might survive.

Chapter 9
BREE

I wake up drowning. Not in water—in pressure. Something pressing against my chest, my throat, my lungs until I can't tell if I'm breathing or suffocating. The dream fades before I can catch it, but the urgency remains, sharp and insistent beneath my ribs.

Get up. Move. Now.

I sit up in the dark, heart hammering against my ribs. The room feels too small, the air too thick. Like the walls are closing in or the ceiling's about to collapse. I need to move. Need to—

The house is too still. That's what's wrong. No creaking floorboards, no distant hum of the refrigerator. Just silence so complete it feels unnatural.

I slide out of bed, bare feet hitting the cool hardwood. Theo's old t-shirt hangs loose on my frame, the soft cotton falling to mid-thigh. I pull the sleeves down over my hands as I step into the hallway. No mist follows me this time. The air feels charged instead, like the moment before lightning strikes.

I pause at the top of the stairs, drawn by the soft murmur of voices drifting up from the kitchen. Low and familiar—the kind of conversation that happens when sleep won't come and company feels necessary. For just a moment, warmth spreads through my chest. Even at four in the morning, they're there for each other.

Then reality crashes back in. They're awake because of me. Because of whatever I've done to them.

I start down the stairs, each step careful and quiet. The voices become clearer as I descend—not words, just the rhythm of conversation that should be comforting but only makes my guilt sharper.

Three sharp knocks on the front door shatter the quiet.

I freeze halfway down the stairs, hand gripping the banister. The knocks weren't loud—more precise than forceful. But they echo through the house like gunshots, making the air itself vibrate.

The voices in the kitchen stop.

My heart kicks against my ribs, not with fear exactly, but with recognition I don't understand. Like some part of me has been waiting for this knock. Expecting it.

Dread pools in my stomach, cold and heavy. Because this is it, isn't it? The confirmation that something really has changed. That whatever's been simmering under the surface—between me, the guys, the air itself—it's not staying hidden anymore.

Whoever's at that door... they already know.

I could call out. Let one of the guys handle this. They'd want to—would insist on it if they knew I was standing here. But something deeper than instinct keeps me moving down the stairs, bare feet silent on the hardwood.

This is for me. I can feel it in my bones.

The front door looms ahead, solid wood that suddenly feels thin as paper. My hand hesitates on the handle, cold metal biting into my palm.

I turn the handle and pull the door open.

Two men stand on the porch, and everything in me goes very still.

The one in front is tall—not just tall, but present in a way that makes the doorframe seem too small to contain him. Dark hair falls across his forehead in careless waves, and his coat hangs open despite the morning chill. He's solid in a way that speaks of strength, of power held in careful check. Every line of his body suggests control, like he's used to being the most dangerous thing in any room.

His eyes find mine and hold—silver-gray and sharp enough to cut. There's assessment there, calculation, but not cruelty. Just the steady gaze of someone taking my measure and finding me... interesting.

I can't tell if he's here to judge me, fight me, or claim me. The thought makes heat crawl up my neck, and I hate how much my body reacts to it.

Behind him stands another man—leaner, smaller, but no less compelling. Where the first radiates controlled power, this one feels like a blade wrapped in silk. His pale hair is styled with deliberate carelessness, and his coat hangs open at the collar, revealing layers that speak of money spent without thought.

He's beautiful in the way that makes you forget to breathe—not soft, but sharp. Dangerous. Like looking directly at something that might burn you if you're not careful.

He's watching me too, but differently. Not assessing—more like I've already answered a question he asked hours ago.

"Who are you?" The words slip out before I can think better of them.

The man in front—the tall one with the predator's stillness—tilts his head slightly. When he speaks, his voice carries an accent I can't place, formal and precise.

"We're here for the one who woke the crown."

Recognition slams into me like a physical blow. That voice. I know that voice. It's the same one that echoed through my bones when I touched the crown, the words I've been replaying endlessly in my mind: Welcome home, Queen of the Mist.

The dread in my stomach crystallizes into certainty. This is real. The crown was real. And now the consequences are standing on my doorstep.

"That's me."

Footsteps echo across the hardwood behind me just as the words leave my mouth. I don't turn around, but I feel them arrive like a wall at my back—Rhett first, then Gray, then the others. They come from the kitchen fast and instinctive, drawn by my voice, by the silence that followed the knock.

The pale man's gaze flicks from me to the protective wall of men behind me, then back to my face, and I catch the ghost of a smile.

Their presence surrounds me, not loud but undeniable. The air shifts, charged with a tension that has nothing to do with magic and everything to do with five men ready to stand between me and whatever waits on the other side of that threshold.

The tall stranger's eyes take us all in with clinical precision. When his gaze returns to me, there's something that might be pity in his expression.

"You don't even know what you are, do you?"

The words sting because they're true. But before I can respond, the man behind him speaks for the first time.

"She doesn't have to know." His voice is lighter than his companion's, but no less compelling. "She's already doing it."

As if summoned by his words, mist begins to curl around my ankles. Not thick or dramatic—just a whisper of silver that drifts toward the open door like it's curious about our visitors.

The pale man's eyes track its movement with interest. The dark one doesn't react at all.

"I'm Thane," the tall stranger says, his silver gaze still holding mine. "This is Stellan. Can we come in? We have a lot to discuss."

The request hangs in the air between us, heavy with implications I don't understand but can feel in my bones. Behind me, the air tightens. The kind of tension that says someone's about to step between me and the unknown—even if I haven't asked them to.

But the dread in my stomach has shifted into something else. Not acceptance exactly, but resignation. This was always going to happen. The moment I touched that crown, this became inevitable.

I step back, opening the door wider despite the sharp intake of breath from someone behind me.

"Come in."

Chapter 10
BREE

I step aside to let them in, my bare feet suddenly cold against the hardwood. The formal living room looms to our left, but I can't face the idea of sitting across from these strangers in a space that feels too big, too empty.

"Kitchen," I say, the word slipping out before I can think better of it. Where things feel... safer.

Thane's silver eyes flick to mine, but he doesn't argue. Just nods once and follows as I lead them toward the back of the house.

The guys fall in behind me, their tension radiating through the air like heat. I can feel their unease, their protective instincts kicking in, but they're following my lead. For now.

As we approach the kitchen, Theo catches my eye. There's something in his expression—that quiet intensity that's always steadied me, but also a question. Like he's asking if I'm okay, if I need him to step in.

I reach out, fingertips brushing his wrist. "I don't know what questions to ask," I whisper, the admission slipping out raw and honest.

His expression softens immediately. "I've got you," he says quietly, and something in my chest loosens slightly.

Jace immediately moves toward the coffee maker, needing something to do with his hands. "Coffee?" he asks, already pulling out mugs. "Water? I think we've got some of those fancy tea bags Theo bought."

Rhett shoots him a look that could melt steel. The last thing we need is to play host to whatever these men are.

Gray positions himself near the window where he can see everything. Rhett claims his usual spot by the counter, arms crossed, radiating barely contained tension.

I move toward the table, drawn to the empty chair next to Wes. He's sitting straighter than usual, but something about his posture seems off. Careful. When I approach, he goes completely still without looking at me.

I settle into the chair beside him, and that's when I feel it.

A pull. Gentle but insistent, like invisible threads trying to draw me closer. The air between us feels charged, different. My skin tingles where we're close but not quite touching.

Thane and Stellan take the remaining chairs. Stellan lounges with casual elegance while Thane sits straight, every line of his body suggesting controlled power. When he speaks, his voice carries an authority that makes me want to shrink into myself.

"Gray," he says, silver gaze finding him immediately. "Shifter." He tilts his head slightly, considering. "Though I haven't seen your kind in a long time."

Gray goes rigid against the wall, his face draining of color.

"Rhett. Fire Warden."

Rhett's hands clench into fists, and I swear I see heat shimmer around his fingers.

"Jace. Airbound."

The mug in Jace's hand shifts slightly in his grip. He stares down at it like it's personally betrayed him.

"Theo. Seer. Still forming, but the threads are there."

Theo's jaw tightens, but he doesn't deny it.

Then Thane's gaze lands on Wes, and his voice drops. Becomes something different.

"And Wes."

He hums low in his throat, a sound that makes my skin prickle. At the same time, Stellan's attention sharpens on Wes with unmistakable recognition. Something passes between them—understanding, maybe, or acknowledgment of something I can't see.

Wes has gone pale, his knuckles white where they grip the table. He still won't meet anyone's eyes.

"What does that mean?" The question bursts out of me before I can stop it. "What are you saying about them?"

Thane's gaze returns to me, and for a moment, something like disbelief flashes across his face. "You really don't know," he says, more observation than question. His tone sharpens, but he doesn't pause. "What you are. What you've awakened."

"No, I don't." My voice cracks slightly. "That's why I need you to explain it."

"The Ether doesn't just return," Stellan says, his voice carrying dark amusement. "It transforms everything around it. Everyone."

The mist stirs at my ankles, responding to the spike of panic in my chest. "You're saying I did this to them?"

"You're saying she hurt us?" Rhett's voice cuts through the air like a blade, protective fury radiating from every line of his body.

"Not hurt," Thane corrects, his tone carefully neutral. "Awakened. Magic was always there, dormant. Sleeping. Your power simply... reminded it how to wake up."

My stomach drops. "So this is my fault."

"No," Theo says quietly, but with certainty. "It's not fault. It's change. And you didn't choose it any more than we did. But we *can* choose what happens next."

I look at him gratefully, remembering why I asked for his help in the first place.

"But also," he continues, addressing Thane directly. "We need to understand what comes next."

Guilt still churns in my chest as I look around at them—these five men who've been my anchors, my family, my everything. And now they're changing because of me.

"What happens now?" I whisper.

"Now," Thane says, leaning forward slightly, "we discuss why this place isn't safe anymore." His jaw tics, just barely, like the admission costs him something.

Ice slides down my spine. "What do you mean?"

"Power like yours doesn't go unnoticed. The Council felt your awakening. Others did too." His silver eyes hold mine, and I see genuine concern there. "Not all of them will be as... diplomatic as we are."

"There's a place," Stellan adds, studying his nails with deliberate casualness. "Connected to your bloodline. Your sanctuary."

"My what?"

"It was abandoned," Thane continues. "Forgotten. But the foundations remain. The protections."

"And now?" The question slips out, though I'm not sure I want the answer.

"Now it's being prepared for your return." That small tic in his jaw again.

The weight of his words settles over the kitchen like a storm cloud. I look around at the guys—Gray's jaw is tight, Rhett's hands are clenched, Jace is frozen with the coffee pot halfway to the mugs. And Wes... Wes is staring at Stellan with something that looks like recognition.

The mist curls thicker around my ankles, and I realize my hands are shaking. I grip the edge of the table to ground myself, but the wood feels different under my fingers—warped somehow, like the whole world is shifting around me and I'm just now catching up.

"I don't understand any of this," I admit, hating how small my voice sounds. "I just... I need time to think."

"Of course," Thane replies, but there's something in his tone that suggests time isn't something we have much of.

The kitchen falls quiet except for the soft hum of the refrigerator and the sound of my own racing heartbeat.

Everything's changing, and I don't know how to stop it.

I'm not even sure I want to.

Chapter 11
WES

Everyone's pretending to process what just happened, but the silence in the kitchen is suffocating.

Jace fidgets with his coffee mug.

Rhett's jaw looks like it might crack from the tension.

Gray hasn't moved from his spot by the window, but his knuckles are white where they grip the sill.

And me?

I'm fixating on one thing.

Why didn't Thane say what I am?

He went around the room like he was reading from some cosmic registry.

Gray—Shifter.

Rhett—Fire Warden.

Jace—Airbound.

Theo—Seer.

Each of them got a title. A classification. Something to hold onto.

Then he looked at me and said... Wes.

Just my name. Nothing else. Like I'm an unfinished sentence no one wants to write down.

Did he not know?

Did he know and choose not to say it in front of the others?

Does Stellan know?

The questions spiral faster than I can catch them, and I feel that familiar emptiness clawing at my chest again. The hunger that food doesn't touch, that sleep doesn't ease.

"So..."

Jace breaks the silence, voice strained with forced humor. "Anyone else feel like we just got sorted into magical Hogwarts houses and one of us didn't make the list?"

The joke falls flat. No one even smiles.

I push back from the table, chair scraping too loud across the floor. "Need a minute," I mutter, already turning toward the hallway.

No one stops me.

But I feel someone watching me go—probably Theo, always watching with eyes that see too much.

The hallway is cooler. Quieter.

I slip beneath the staircase, shoulders pressed to the wall like the wood might hold me together.

My breath comes fast and shallow. I close my eyes and try not to feel anything.

The hunger is worse now. More insistent. Like it's been waiting for me to be alone so it can stop pretending to be polite.

I press a hand to my throat, where the glow started. Rub it like I can make it disappear.

But it's still there. Warmth under my skin that doesn't belong.

What if it's worse than they think?

What if I'm not like them at all?

What if it's not a gift?

The thoughts come sharp, each one slicing a little deeper.

Maybe that's why Thane didn't name it. Maybe there isn't a pretty title for whatever I'm becoming.

Footsteps echo down the hall. Light. Deliberate.

I tense.

"It has a way of getting under your skin, doesn't it?"

Stellan's voice cuts clean through the dark.

He leans against the doorframe like he's been waiting for this moment.

All that elegance, effortless and dangerous.

I don't answer.

Can't.

Because he's right, and we both know it.

He doesn't push.

Just watches me with those razor eyes, taking in my posture, my breathing, the way I'm braced like the walls are the only thing keeping me upright.

"You've been starving for days," he says simply. "It's not food you need. And it won't stop."

The words hit like a punch to the ribs.

"You don't know anything about me."

"Don't I?"

His head tilts. He studies me like a riddle he's already solved.

"Incubus-class Feeder. Same as me."

The air leaves my lungs in a rush.

"That's not—"

"Possible? Real?"

He huffs a breath. Might be a laugh.

"Tell me, Wes—when was the last time you felt full? Actually full?"

I say nothing. Because I haven't.

Not since the crown. Maybe not ever.

"We don't take," Stellan says. "Not the in way you think. We feel. We amplify. We get drunk on emotion if we're not careful."

"I don't want this."

The words tear out of me. Raw.

"I don't want to feed off people."

"You already are."

He says it without cruelty. Without softness. Just fact.

"You're just doing it wrong."

"Wrong how?"

"You're fighting it. Starving yourself into being human."

He steps closer. The air shifts.

"I've seen our kind shatter from the inside trying to pretend they're normal."

Something in his voice makes me look up.

"You think I liked it?" he says, quieter now. "Waking up starving in a world that didn't believe in what I was? Needing something everyone else was afraid to name?"

I don't answer.

Because he's not wrong.

"You're lucky," he murmurs. "You've got her. You've got them. The Ether won't let you rot in denial. But it *will* hurt you if you keep trying to resist it."

He steps even closer—not threatening. Not seductive. Just... present.

Close enough that I feel it.

The weight of him. The stillness. The hum of shared hunger.

My pulse spikes.

The hunger... eases. Not gone. But acknowledged. Like it exhaled.

Stellan smiles faintly.

Not cruel. Not kind. Just knowing.

"You'll feel it more around her. Around them."

His eyes flick toward the hallway.

"Especially him."

I freeze. "What do you mean?"

But he's already moving. Already retreating, that smirk back on his lips.

"You'll figure it out. Or you'll break trying."

He pauses in the doorway, gives me one last glance.

"Either way... I'm here."

Then he's gone.

Gone, and I'm left in the quiet with only my breath and the ache that still gnaws at my ribs.

I slide down the wall, head in my hands.

The hunger hasn't faded.

The fear hasn't left.

But for the first time since this started, I know I'm not the only one carrying this.

It's not food I need.

But gods help me—

I don't know what else to want.

Chapter 12
GRAY

The kitchen feels hollow after Wes leaves.

Not empty—the others are still here, voices drifting in muted conversation as they process whatever the hell just happened. Thane sits like carved from stone, radiating the kind of controlled power that makes my teeth ache. Bree hovers near the table, her fingers tracing patterns in the wood grain while the mist curls restlessly around her ankles.

But something's missing. Someone's missing.

And it's not just that Wes walked out.

It's the way he walked out. Like something was clawing its way under his skin. Like he was one breath away from breaking apart in front of all of us.

I've seen Wes afraid before. Seen him angry, hurt, lost. But I've never seen him look like prey.

My hands flex against my thighs, an restless energy building in my chest that has nothing to do with magic and everything to do with instinct. The kind that says something's wrong. That says I should move. Should follow.

Should hunt.

The thought stops me cold.

Hunt?

Where the hell did that come from?

"Gray?" Theo's voice cuts through the fog in my head. "You okay?"

I blink, realizing I've been staring at the doorway where Wes disappeared. The others are watching me with varying degrees of concern—even Thane's silver gaze has sharpened slightly.

"Fine," I mutter, pushing back from the table. "Need some air."

It's not entirely a lie. The kitchen suddenly feels too small, too crowded. Like the walls are pressing in and I can't quite catch my breath.

I move toward the hallway, telling myself I'm just going outside. Getting space. Not following Wes like some kind of—

The scent hits me before I reach the hall.

Not blood. Not fear. Something deeper. Richer. Like emotion distilled into heat. Like hunger given shape.

My vision sharpens without warning, the dim hallway suddenly crystal clear. Every shadow, every dust mote, every—

There.

The glow isn't visible, not exactly. But I can feel it radiating from beneath the stairs where Wes has crumpled against the wall. Heat and need and something that makes every protective instinct I've ever had roar to life.

He's not just hungry.

He's starving.

And he's trying so hard to hide it that he's tearing himself apart from the inside.

"—you'll figure it out. Or you'll break trying."

Stellan's voice drifts from the shadows, followed by the soft sound of footsteps retreating. I catch a glimpse of pale hair and that trademark smirk as he disappears around the corner, leaving Wes alone in the dark.

I should go back to the kitchen. Should give Wes space to process whatever just happened between him and Stellan. Should mind my own damn business.

Instead, I step into the hallway.

Wes doesn't look up when I approach. Just stays curled against the wall, head in his hands, shoulders shaking with the effort of holding himself together.

"Hey," I say quietly, settling onto the floor beside him.

He flinches. "I'm fine."

"Bullshit."

That gets me a look—sharp, defensive, raw with something that might be shame. "Gray, I can't—I don't want to—"

"Breathe," I cut him off gently. "Just breathe."

We sit in silence for a moment, and I try to make sense of what I'm feeling. The sharpness in my vision has faded, but the awareness remains. Like I can sense the tension radiating from his skin, the way his pulse hammers against his throat.

Like I'm tuned into something I've never noticed before.

"Stellan told you what you are," I say. It's not a question.

Wes nods without lifting his head. "Feeder. Like him." His voice cracks on the words. "I don't want to be like him."

"You're not."

"You don't know that."

"Yeah, I do." I lean back against the wall, mirroring his position. "Because you're sitting here hating yourself for being hungry instead of taking what you need."

Wes finally looks at me, confusion flickering across his face. "What's that supposed to mean?"

I study him for a moment—the shadows under his eyes, the way his hands shake slightly where they rest on his knees. The careful distance he's maintaining even though every line of his body screams for contact.

"How long have you been starving, Wes?"

He doesn't answer. Doesn't need to. The truth is written all over his face.

"Take what you need," I say quietly.

He goes rigid. "I don't even know how."

"I know." I shift slightly, close enough for him to feel the warmth between us. "That's not what I'm offering."

He blinks. "Then what?"

"Permission." I let the word settle between us. "To stop fighting it. To stop hating yourself for something you never asked for. To figure this out... with someone who isn't afraid of you."

Something flickers across his face—hope mixed with terror. "I don't know what I am. What I need. What any of this means."

"Doesn't matter." I meet his eyes, steady. "Bree wouldn't want you to starve. And I'm not going to let you do this alone."

The mention of her name hits him hard. His breath catches, and for a moment, I see through the careful walls he's built. See the guilt, the fear, the bone-deep certainty that he's becoming something dangerous.

"She's not here," he whispers.

"So?"

"So how can I—" Wes stops, his throat working around the words. "How can I want this when she's not here? When I don't even understand what the hell I'm becoming?"

There's something unraveling in him—not fear exactly, but grief twisted into guilt.

"And because," Wes says, voice rough, almost bitter, "I'm scared."

He swallows, like the words hurt to say.

"Scared I'll lose control. Scared I'll take too much. Scared that just... *wanting from her* makes me dangerous. After everything she's already been through."

His voice breaks—just slightly.

"Gods, Gray." A whisper. A confession.

"Gods, how I want her."

It lands like a punch to the chest. Not because it's new. But because he finally said it.

Finally said what we've all been afraid to say.

I let the silence breathe between us. Let him feel it, instead of running from it.

"That's not weakness," I say. "It's restraint."

He shakes his head. "But what if it's not enough?"

"Then you get better. You *learn* control. You do the work now—so when she's ready, you're not afraid of yourself."

He stares at me, raw and exposed. And I know that look, because I've worn it.

"You think I don't feel it too?" I say quietly. "You think I haven't imagined what it would be like to touch her and not have her flinch? To kiss her without holding back?"

Something flickers in Wes's eyes. Not challenge. Not jealousy.

Recognition.

"You're not afraid of me," he says, and there's wonder in his voice.

"Should I be?"

The question hangs between us, heavy with implications I'm not sure either of us is ready to name. But I don't take it back. Don't look away.

Because the truth is, I'm not afraid. If anything, I feel... drawn. Like there's something in him calling to something in me, and I've spent years pretending not to hear it.

The hunger doesn't disappear from his eyes. But it shifts. Becomes something softer. More human.

"Gray," he starts, voice rough with emotion.

I don't know what he's going to say. Don't get the chance to find out.

Because suddenly he's moving, closing the distance between us with desperate urgency. His mouth finds mine—fast, intense, not practiced or polished. Just need made real.

The kiss is electric. Not in the cheesy, romance novel way. In the way that makes my vision go white at the edges, makes something deep in my chest roar with satisfaction. Like puzzle pieces clicking into place. Like coming home.

He pulls back almost immediately, eyes wide with panic.

"I'm sorry—fuck—I shouldn't have—"

"Hey." I catch his wrist gently, anchor him before he can spiral. "You're not the only one trying to figure it out."

The words surprise me as much as they seem to surprise him. But they're true. Whatever this is—this pull between us, this awareness that's been building since the crown changed everything—I'm feeling it too.

"I don't know what I'm doing," Wes admits, his voice small.

"Neither do I." I brush my thumb over his wrist, feeling his pulse race under my touch. "But I know you're not broken. And I know you don't have to figure it out alone."

Something in his expression cracks open. Relief, maybe. Because he finally heard me this time.

The hunger is still there—I can feel it radiating from his skin like heat. But it's different now. Acknowledged instead of denied. Shared instead of hidden.

"What happens now?" he asks.

I don't have an answer for that. Don't know what any of this means or where it leads. All I know is that sitting here with him feels right in a way nothing has since Bree disappeared.

"Now we go back," I say finally. "And we figure out how to help her. Together."

Wes nods slowly, some of the tension finally leaving his shoulders. When he stands, I follow, and for a moment we just look at each other in the dim hallway.

"Thank you," he says quietly.

I want to tell him he doesn't need to thank me. Want to explain that I'd do it again in a heartbeat, that something in me wants to keep doing it until he never feels empty again.

Instead, I just nod.

Because some things don't need words yet.

Some things just need time.

Chapter 13
BREE

The kitchen felt too small after everything Thane and Stellan revealed. Too many eyes watching, too many questions I don't have answers for. I told them I needed to lie down—not entirely a lie. My head throbs with the weight of names I don't understand: Scarborne, Council, sanctuary.

But instead of going to my room, I find myself in the upstairs hallway, drawn to the place where everything changed.

I don't mean to go back to the door. My feet take me anyway.

The door looks ordinary now. Just painted wood and tarnished brass, hiding cleaning supplies and cobwebs like it always has. Like the impossible room beyond never existed. Like I imagined the crown, the voice, the way the mist sang when I touched ancient metal.

But I didn't imagine it. I can still feel the echo in my chest—not pain exactly, but awareness. Like something sleeping has cracked one eye open and is watching.

The second my fingers brush the wood grain, the air shifts.

Something remembers me.

And something responds.

The sigil blooms to life beneath my palm, glowing faint as breath fog on glass, then brighter. Silver lines trace patterns that hurt to look at directly—not because they're harsh, but because they're familiar in a way that makes no sense. Like trying to remember a song from childhood that you've never actually heard.

The Ether slides down my arms, drawn to the mark like iron filings to a magnet. I watch, fascinated and terrified, as tendrils of mist rise from my skin to dance around the glowing symbol.

I did this. Somehow, without thinking, without trying—I called it back.

"Do you know what that is?"

The voice cuts through the stillness, quiet and unreadable. I spin around to find Thane at the top of the stairs, silver eyes fixed on the sigil—not on me. His usual controlled composure has cracked slightly, revealing something I don't fully recognize.

Hunger, maybe. Or fear.

"No," I say, pulling my hand back. The light fades but doesn't disappear entirely. "I don't know what any of this is."

He moves closer, each step deliberate. "That mark... I've seen drawings of it. Sketches in books older than kingdoms." His gaze flicks to mine. "But never real. Never responding."

"Responding to what?"

"To you." He stops just out of arm's reach, close enough that I can see the sharp angles of his face in the sigil's dying light. "You shouldn't be able to reveal that. That magic is sealed to bloodline."

"I didn't reveal it," I say, defensive. "It responded."

Something flickers across his expression—surprise, maybe, or recognition. "That's what makes it dangerous."

The word sits heavy between us. Dangerous. Like I'm something to be contained, controlled, eliminated.

"Is that why you're really here?" The question slips out before I can stop it. "To decide if I'm dangerous?"

He doesn't answer immediately. Just studies me with those unsettling silver eyes, like he's trying to solve a puzzle that keeps changing shape.

"I was sent," he says finally, "to investigate the surge. To assess the threat."

"And did you volunteer?" I press.

Silence. Which is answer enough.

"So what's your assessment?" I wrap my arms around myself, suddenly cold. "Am I the threat you were expecting?"

"No." The admission seems to surprise him as much as it surprises me. "You're something else entirely."

"What's that supposed to mean?"

Thane leans against the wall, some of the formal distance leaving his posture. For a moment, he looks almost... tired. "I expected someone power-hungry. Someone who would try to use their awakening to claim what they thought they deserved." His gaze finds mine. "Instead, I find someone who's spent weeks trying to convince herself she doesn't deserve anything at all."

The observation hits harder than it should. "You don't know me."

"Don't I?" He tilts his head slightly. "You're afraid of your own power. Afraid of hurting the people you love. You'd rather run than risk being the thing that destroys their happiness."

Heat crawls up my neck. "Stop."

"You want to know why I care?" His voice drops, becomes something rougher. "Because if you're real—if you're what I think you are—then everything changes. The Council, the balance of power, the way magic itself works in this realm."

"What if I don't want it?" The words tear out of me, raw and desperate. "What if I just want to be normal? To have a normal life with normal problems?"

"That won't stop it."

The certainty in his voice makes my stomach drop. "Then what am I supposed to do?"

"Learn what you are before someone else decides for you."

The mist stirs around my ankles, responding to the spike of anxiety in my chest. Thane's gaze tracks its movement, and something in his expression shifts. Becomes almost... hungry.

"They'll come for you," he says quietly. "Others like me. Others worse than me. And they won't care what you want or don't want. They'll see power, and they'll try to take it."

"And you?" I meet his eyes, needing to understand. "What do you see?"

He's quiet for a long moment, silver gaze searching my face. When he speaks, his voice is barely above a whisper.

"I see someone who could change everything. And someone who's terrified of that responsibility."

The sigil pulses once more, bright enough to cast shadows, then fades back to ordinary wood. Like whatever magic called it forth has decided we've said enough for now.

I should go. Should put distance between myself and this conversation that feels too big, too heavy. Should hide in my room and pretend none of this is real.

Instead, I find myself asking, "Have you ever wanted something you knew would destroy you?"

The question catches him off guard. For just a moment, his careful mask slips, and I see something raw underneath. Something that looks almost... vulnerable.

"Every day," he admits.

The honesty in his voice does something to my chest. Makes the space between us feel charged with more than just magic. Like we're circling around truths neither of us is ready to speak.

"Then I guess I'd better figure out what I am," I say finally, "before someone else does."

I turn to go, needing distance before I say something I can't take back. But I only make it a few steps before the air behind me stirs.

I glance back.

Silver mist curls around Thane's boots—slow and quiet, like fog rolling in on instinct. It brushes the hem of his coat, lingers there a beat too long.

He doesn't move.

His eyes widen—just barely—but I see it. A flicker of something raw behind all that control. Like he felt it too.

I frown, chest tight.

The Ether isn't supposed to do that. Not with anyone else.

So why does it look like it's reaching for him?

The mist pulls back slowly, reluctantly, and drifts toward me like nothing happened. But I catch the way Thane's breath catches, the way his hands clench at his sides.

And just before I disappear into my room, I hear him whisper something that makes my heart stutter.

"Brielle."

Not Bree. Not the name everyone else uses.

Brielle.

Like he knows something about me that I don't know about myself

Chapter 14
JACE

The kitchen feels like a graveyard after everyone scatters. Theo's hunched over his laptop, typing like he's trying to escape through the keyboard. Rhett leans against the counter, staring out the window at nothing, his jaw working like he's chewing on words he can't say.

And me? I'm standing here like an idiot, trying to figure out how everything went sideways so fast.

"Well," I say, aiming for my usual lightness, "pretty sure they're gonna replace us with council guys who wear silk and smirk for a living."

The joke falls flat. Hits the floor and dies there.

Rhett doesn't even glance my way. Theo stops typing.

"Then stop acting like you're expendable."

The words slice through the air, sharp enough to draw blood. Theo doesn't look up from his screen, but there's steel in his voice I've never heard before. Cold and cutting and aimed right at my chest.

The silence that follows feels sharp enough to choke on.

I blink, caught off guard by the sudden venom. "What's that supposed to mean?"

"You know exactly what it means." Theo's fingers have gone still on the keyboard, but he still won't look at me. "You deflect with jokes every time something gets real. Like you're afraid if you stop being funny for five seconds, we'll realize we don't need you."

The words hit like a sucker punch. My throat tightens, but I force out a laugh that sounds hollow even to me. "Jesus, Theo. Tell me how you really feel."

That finally gets him to look up. His dark eyes are sharp with frustration, but there's something else there too. Something that looks almost like regret.

"Jace, wait—"

"Nah." I shake my head, already backing toward the door. "It's fine. Really. Message received loud and clear."

I'm out of the kitchen before either of them can say another word, my heart hammering against my ribs like it's trying to escape. The hallway feels too narrow, like the walls are closing in and I can't quite catch my breath.

Expendable.

The word echoes in my head, mixing with Theo's voice until I can't tell which one's worse—hearing it or knowing he's probably right.

I need air. Need space. Need to move before I do something stupid like punch a wall or break down in the middle of the hallway where anyone might see.

The back door slams harder than I mean it to as I step outside, cold air hitting my overheated skin like a slap. The yard is quiet, empty, just shadows and moonlight stretching across the grass. Better than the suffocating weight of concern inside.

I grab my throwing knives from where I stashed them by the door—old habit from when we were kids and I needed somewhere to put my restless energy. The familiar weight of the blades in my hands is grounding, real in a way nothing else feels right now.

If I can't be magical, I can at least be sharp.

The first knife flies true, embedding in the old oak with a satisfying thunk. The second follows, then the third. Fast, angry throws that dare something—anything—to come at me.

But as I settle into the rhythm, something starts to shift.

The fourth knife veers slightly midair, correcting its trajectory in a way that shouldn't be possible. I feel the air shift around me, just enough to raise goosebumps.

Weird.

I pull another blade, focus harder this time. The throw is perfect—too perfect. The knife hangs in the air for just a beat too long before embedding itself exactly where I aimed.

My breathing picks up, not from exertion but from something else. Something that makes my skin prickle and the air around me feel... different.

"Not now," I mutter, wiping sweat from my forehead. "Not tonight."

But even as I say it, I can feel something stirring in my chest. Like a door I didn't know existed has cracked open, and whatever's on the other side is trying to get out.

I throw the rest of the knives in quick succession, each one finding its mark with impossible precision. When I'm done, I stand there breathing hard, staring at the perfect pattern they've made in the bark.

That's not normal. That's not *human*.

But I don't have the energy to deal with whatever this is. Not tonight. Not when Theo's words are still echoing in my head, cutting deeper than any blade ever could.

I collect the knives in silence, shoving them back into their sheaths with more force than necessary. The house looms ahead, warm light spilling from the windows like a promise I'm not sure I deserve.

As I slip back through the door, the familiar sounds of home wash over me—the hum of the refrigerator, the creak of old floorboards, the distant murmur of voices from upstairs. It should be comforting. Instead, it just reminds me how easy it would be for all of this to disappear.

How easy it would be for them to realize they don't need me.

I'm halfway to my room when I hear it—Bree's voice, soft and muffled, drifting from behind her door. She's not alone. Theo's voice answers, too quiet for me to make out words but unmistakably his.

I should keep walking. Should give them privacy. Should mind my own damn business.

Instead, I slow my steps, drawn by the need to know something, anything about what's really going on.

"I called work," Bree is saying, her voice barely audible through the wood. "Told them I needed more time."

Theo says something I can't catch, his tone gentle but serious.

"I know," Bree replies. "But I can't ask them to come with me. I can't ask any of you to uproot your lives just because mine is falling apart." Her voice cracks slightly. "I've already taken enough from all of you just by existing."

The words hit me like a physical blow, stealing the air from my lungs. *Taken from us?* She thinks she's taken something from us?

Theo's response is too quiet to hear, but whatever he says makes Bree laugh—bitter and broken.

"Maybe. But that doesn't make it fair."

I step back from the door, my chest tight with emotions I don't want to feel. She's not trying to leave us behind. She's trying not to take us down with her.

But she doesn't understand. Doesn't realize that we're already gone. That we crossed that line years ago and there's no going back.

My fists clench at my sides as I retreat to my room, Theo's words and Bree's pain mixing together into something sharp and jagged in my chest.

Expendable.

Maybe I am. Maybe we all are, in the face of whatever's coming for her. But I'd follow her anyway. Into whatever mess she thinks she's dragging us toward.

Gods help me, I already have.

Chapter 15
THEO

The kitchen hums with ordinary evening energy, but something feels off-balance.

Bree stands at the stove making dinner, stirring cheese sauce with absent movements while her mind clearly wanders elsewhere. She's been quiet since we spoke this afternoon in her room, processing everything Thane and Stellan revealed. Jace sets the table with restless energy, silverware clinking against plates as he moves. Rhett organizes tomorrow's work supplies by the back door—mundane tasks that feel necessary when everything else feels uncertain.

Gray leans against the counter, ostensibly reading something on his phone but really watching Bree like he's cataloging every small change in her expression.

I notice all of it, the careful distances and unspoken tensions. But what draws my attention most is the way the Ether flickers around Bree's ankles—restless, aware, responding to thoughts she's not sharing.

It's not fear, I think, watching silver tendrils curl and retreat. *It's anticipation. Like it knows something we don't.*

I'm drying dishes when the vision hits.

Sharp and sudden, yanking me out of the kitchen and into something that feels more real than the plate slipping from my hands.

The six of us walking away from the house. Morning light too bright, too quiet. Bree moving toward something old and half-buried in overgrowth—stone foundations choked with ivy and decades of neglect. Thane walking ahead of us, Stellan at her shoulder like a pale guide. The rest of us following, drawn by something stronger than choice.

Something waits for her there. Not a threat. A memory.

I blink back to the present, breath hitched, the dish towel twisted in my white-knuckled grip. The plate I dropped lies in pieces on the floor.

"Theo?" Bree's voice cuts through the lingering images. "What happened?"

Everyone's looking at me now—Jace pausing mid-reach for another fork, Rhett straightening from his supply sorting, Gray's attention sharp and immediate.

I hesitate, sorting through what I saw versus what I should say. "I had a vision."

The kitchen goes quiet except for the soft bubble of cheese sauce on the stove.

"Of what?" Bree asks, wooden spoon forgotten in her hand.

"Us." I set the towel down carefully, meet her eyes. "Leaving. Tomorrow morning."

"Leaving for where?" Gray's voice carries that edge it gets when he's trying to solve a problem he can't see yet.

"I don't know. Somewhere old. Ruins, maybe. Stone foundations covered in ivy." I look around at their faces, all focused on me with varying degrees of concern and curiosity. "We were all there. Together."

You're sure?" Bree asks, almost whispering.

"Yes." The word tastes strange in my mouth, too heavy to feel like hope. "We're going. All of us.

Before anyone can respond, the front door opens. Thane walks in like he owns the place, silver eyes scanning the kitchen and landing on me with uncomfortable precision.

"Interesting timing," he says, closing the door behind him. "We need to talk."

His gaze lingers on me.

"They're still glowing."

I stiffen. So much for hiding it.

The Ether responds immediately, rising around Bree's legs like it recognizes him.

"About what?" she asks, though something in her tone suggests she already knows.

"About leaving. Tonight, preferably. Tomorrow morning at the latest."

Jace drops the fork he's holding. "Excuse me?"

"The sanctuary," Thane continues, ignoring the interruption. "The place of your bloodline. It's not safe here anymore."

"Because of the Council?" Bree's voice is steadier than it has any right to be.

"Among others." Thane's jaw tightens slightly. "The longer we wait, the more dangerous this becomes. For all of you."

Footsteps echo from the hallway as Stellan appears in the doorway, reading the room with that predatory awareness of his.

Before anyone can ask more questions, Thane's phone rings. He checks the screen, frowns deeply, and steps back outside without a word.

The kitchen holds its breath. Through the glass door, we can see Thane pacing, his free hand gesturing sharply as he speaks in a voice too low to hear.

Then, clear as day:

"Fuck."

Everyone goes still.

I'm halfway to the door when he steps back in, tension bleeding off him in waves. His face is drawn, his usual calm replaced with something colder. Sharper.

"That didn't sound good," Gray says carefully.

Thane doesn't look at him. He looks at Bree.

"The spells around the sanctuary started unraveling the moment you awakened the Ether," he says quietly. "Magical surveillance has already started pinging. The Council's getting closer than I expected."

He exhales, just once. "It's not ready. Not the way I planned."

A long silence.

"Then we don't go?" Jace asks.

"We still go," Thane says, his eyes fixed on Bree. "Because *you* should see it. Because it's yours." His voice softens—just barely—as he adds, "And after that, we'll find somewhere safe."

Stellan, who's been quiet until now, steps into the doorway. "You're not walking into a trap," he says. "You're walking into your inheritance."

The words land heavy in the kitchen's charged air.

I watch Bree process them—see the exact moment she stops thinking like someone who isn't capable, and starts choosing who she wants to be.

The Ether curls higher around her waist, no longer restless but ready. Like it's responding not to pressure, but to her decision.

"Then we go," she says simply.

And just like that, everything changes.

Chapter 16
BREE

The blanket feels wrong in my hands. I sit cross-legged on my bed, turning the soft fabric over in my palms. Jace gave it to me along with all those other things—that overwhelming pile of gifts that made me cry. *"I saw this blanket, and it reminded me of your eyes when you actually smile,"* he'd said, nervous energy making him younger somehow. The memory of his words still makes my chest tight.

But now, holding it, I don't know if I should pack it. Taking it with me to the sanctuary feels like accepting that I'm leaving—*really* leaving. Like I'm choosing them over... what? Over the illusion of independence I've been clinging to?

The house has settled into quiet around me. The others have either gone to bed or drifted into their own spaces to deal with whatever we're all feeling after today. After Theo's vision. After Thane's warning.

After everything changed, again.

The mist curls around my ankles, restless and waiting. It's been doing that all evening—hovering close, like it wants me to say something. To someone. But I don't know what words I'm supposed to find for any of this.

A soft knock interrupts my spiral.

"You still awake?"

Gray's voice, quiet through the door. I hesitate, my grip tightening on the blanket.

"Yeah. Come in."

He steps inside, and I take in the sight of him—hoodie unzipped, sleeves pushed to his elbows, dark hair still damp from the shower. There's something careful in the way he moves, like he's giving me space to change my mind about letting him stay.

He doesn't sit at first. Just studies me the way he always does, like he's trying to read a language he almost knows but doesn't speak out loud.

"Can't decide what to pack?" he asks, nodding toward the blanket.

"Something like that." I smooth my thumb over the stitching, focusing on the texture instead of the knot in my chest. "It feels too real. Like once I put it in a bag, I'm admitting..."

"That you're trusting us," he finishes.

I look up. "I already trust you."

The truth sits lower in my chest, harder to name.

"It's not that," I say softly. "It's admitting this might actually matter. That it's real."

I smooth the blanket in my lap, not looking at him.

"And if we do this—if we really go—"

I glance at him, and the flicker of hope he's trying to hide nearly undoes me.

"It means everything changes."

I swallow.

"For all of us."

He moves closer, settling on the edge of the bed. Not close enough to crowd me, but near enough that I can feel the warmth radiating from his skin.

"Can I ask you something?" The words slip out before I can stop them.

"Always."

I take a breath, steeling myself. "Earlier... when Thane showed up. When he spoke..."

I trail off, but Gray's already watching me closer. His expression shifts, becomes more alert. I pull the blanket higher on my lap, trying to find the courage for what I need to say.

"I recognized his voice. Not just 'I've heard this before'—I *knew* it. I felt it in my chest. Like he was there, the night of the crown. Inside the light. Inside me."

My voice drops to barely a whisper. "He's the one who called me Queen of the Mist. I'm sure of it."

The silence stretches between us. Gray doesn't speak right away, but something shifts behind his eyes. Not surprise—something closer to confirmation.

"You haven't told the others," he says finally.

"No. I don't even know if it means anything." I shake my head, frustration bleeding into my voice. "But I can't shake the feeling that he's been in this longer than he's admitting. That he's not just some Council representative who showed up because of the surge."

"It means something," Gray says, and there's certainty in his voice. "You feel like he was in that moment—like he helped create it?"

I nod, the admission feeling like stepping off a cliff. "I haven't even told them what the voice said. I didn't want it to be real."

"And now?"

"Now I think he's been watching. Planning. And I think he knows exactly what he's doing." The mist coils tighter near my feet, protective and tense. "I don't want him in my head. I don't want him in that memory."

Gray leans forward, his voice low and steady. "If he was in that moment—if he called you queen—then maybe he wasn't just witnessing your awakening. Maybe he's part of what caused it."

The possibility terrifies me, but it doesn't feel impossible. Nothing feels impossible anymore.

"And if that's true," Gray continues, "we don't know what else he can do."

I close my eyes, trying to process the implications. When I open them again, Gray is still watching me with that unflinching steadiness that's always been his strength.

"I'll keep it between us," he says quietly. "But Bree..."

"Yeah?"

"If he was there—if he's been in your head—then we anchor it. Right here, right now. You told me. And I'll carry it."

Something warm unfurls in my chest. "Just you?"

"Just me."

The mist stirs, and for a moment, the weight of the secret feels shared instead of crushing.

"Can I tell you something I haven't told you before?" Gray asks.

I nod, curiosity overtaking the lingering fear.

He goes quiet, his hands clasped between his knees. His gaze drops to the floor.

When he speaks, it's more to the space between us than to me.

"A few days ago, after you touched the crown, I had this dream. Except it wasn't a dream. It was a memory. But not mine." His eyes meet mine, and there's something vulnerable and terrified in them. "I was yours, Bree. Your memory of the night your mother left. I felt what you felt that night. I was at your window, banging on the glass, watching her walk away. I felt your heart breaking. I felt how alone you were."

The violation of it hits first—someone was inside my most private moment, one of my worst memories. My breath goes tight. My throat closes. For a split second, I want to run.

But then...

"It was you," I breathe. The fear shifts into something else. Relief, maybe. "If it had to be anyone..."

"I'm sorry," Gray says quickly. "I didn't mean for it to happen. I didn't ask for it."

"I know." I wrap my arms around myself. "You remember everything? How it felt?"

He nods, and I see it—my childhood pain reflected back at me through his eyes. Not perfectly. Not fully. But real.

"I told you guys about that night," I say quietly. "We were just kids. I remember crying about it to all of you."

"You told us she left," Gray says. "But not like that."

His voice softens.

"Not what it felt like. Not what it did to you."

He hesitates, then:

"I don't think I ever understood why you kept so much in until now. Not all of it. But maybe... maybe this was part of it."

He shifts slightly, glancing at the mist. Then back at me.

"There's something else," he says. "From that night. Not a memory I borrowed. Mine."

I blink. "What do you mean?"

"When I looked out my window... there was a glow. Faint. Like fog, but not. It was around her. Your mom. Just for a second. Like the night swallowed her—but left something behind. I thought maybe I imagined it. Or maybe it was just the streetlights."

His voice drops.

"But it looked like this."

He glances at the mist still drifting near my feet.

"It looked like you."

The admission hangs between us, impossibly heavy.

He's not just talking about the memory I gave him. This part—this glow—this is his. His memory. His eyes. His truth.

Something about that makes it harder to breathe.

But also easier to believe.

The mist stirs—lifting, faint and deliberate. It curls gently toward Gray and brushes against his shoe. I see it, but I don't call it back.

Gray looks down at the mist, then up at me.

"Everything changed the moment she walked away."

"Everything changed the moment you lived it with me," I say, the words feeling strange and true all at once.

Gray doesn't answer right away.

Something flickers across his face—something he doesn't say.

Not denial. Not guilt. Just... weight.

I tilt my head, watching him. "It wasn't just you, was it?"

His shoulders rise, then fall. Barely a breath.

He doesn't lie. But he doesn't answer either.

"Everything changed," I murmur, "the moment I wasn't the only one carrying it anymore."

He stands and crosses to the window, his movements quiet, unsettled.

I join him there, and we stand side by side, both of us understanding now that something impossible has been happening between us.

"I'm not sorry it happened, Bree. Even if it hurt. Even if it wasn't mine to feel." He turns to look at me. "Because now I know. Really know. And you don't have to carry it alone anymore."

"I think we've both been carrying ghosts," I say.

"Maybe they brought us here."

The silence that follows isn't empty or sad. It's full of understanding, of secrets finally shared. The mist settles around our feet, no longer restless.

Gray turns to face me, and something in his expression makes my heart skip.

"Thank you," I say. "For seeing me. Even then."

He nods, voice barely above a whisper. "I never stopped."

I look down at the blanket still clutched in my hands. The decision feels easier now, with Gray's quiet presence beside me and the weight of shared truth between us.

I fold the blanket carefully and set it on the pile of clothes I'm taking to the sanctuary.

Some things are worth carrying with you.

Some people are worth trusting.

And some secrets are meant to be shared in the dark, with mist curling around your feet and the promise that you don't have to carry the ghosts alone anymore.

Chapter 17
BREE

The house is silent, but I'm louder now. Inside. Awake in ways I don't know how to hush. I've been packed for an hour, maybe two. Everything I'm taking to the sanctuary fits in one small bag—clothes, the blanket Gray helped me choose, my mother's ring. It's not much, but it feels like everything.

The mist curls around my ankles as I sit on the edge of the bed, restless and waiting. Not anxious. Not afraid. Just... full. Too full to rest, too alert to sleep.

I glance at the blanket one more time where it sits folded on top of my bag. Not longing—just anchoring. A reminder that some things are worth carrying with you.

The mist parts for me as I stand, then curls back around my ankles like it forgot to let go. It tugs gently toward the door, curious but not forceful. I don't follow it on purpose, but I find myself walking barefoot down the hall, through the quiet house, toward the back door.

Dawn hasn't broken yet, but the sky is lighter now. That soft gray that comes before sunrise, when the world feels suspended between night and day.

That's when I see him.

Jace stands in the backyard, facing the old oak tree. His hoodie is zipped tight against the morning chill, and there's something sharp and controlled about the way he moves. He draws his arm back and releases—a knife flying straight and true into the bark.

Another blade follows. Then another.

His movements are practiced, too practiced. Like he's not calming down—he's holding back. His jaw is tight, shoulders tense despite the fluid precision of each throw.

I watch from the doorway, unseen at first. There's something beautiful about the way he moves, but also something desperate. Like he's trying to prove something to himself with every perfect strike.

"You're up early," I say quietly.

He throws another knife without looking at me. "Didn't sleep."

"Did you ever?"

That gets him to glance over. There's a half-smile on his lips, but it doesn't stick. Doesn't reach his eyes.

"You heading out?" he asks, nodding toward my bare feet. "Seems a little early for a nature walk."

"I don't know. Just... walking."

"You always walk toward knives?"

I step closer anyway, drawn by something in his voice. Something that sounds like the edge of breaking.

"This place never felt like home," I say softly. "Not to me.

He doesn't look at me, but he stills.

"But you..." I swallow. "You were the first one who made me feel like I belonged."

He goes stiller. Quieter.

"And I think you still don't believe you do."

His shoulders tense, the knife frozen in his grip. He doesn't deny it, which tells me everything.

"Jace."

When he finally looks at me, there's something raw in his green eyes. Vulnerable in a way that makes my chest ache.

I step into his space slowly—not to take, but to offer.

"You don't have to say anything," I whisper. "I just wanted you to know—before we go." I reach up, my fingers barely brushing his jaw. "You belong. To us. To me."

His breath catches.

And then I rise onto my toes and kiss him—not because I'm overwhelmed, but because I *mean it*. Because I want him to *feel* it.

He doesn't move at first. Doesn't even breathe.

Then slowly, carefully, his hand finds my waist.

And he kisses me back like it's the first real thing he's been given in a long, long time.

I feel the mist gather around us, low and slow, not flaring—just folding inward like it wants to hold the moment still. Like it knows this matters.

When I pull back, Jace stares at me like he's seeing something he didn't know he was allowed to hope for.

"What was that for?" he asks. Not defensive—just raw. Honest.

"So you wouldn't forget," I answer.

His thumb brushes across my cheek, so gentle it almost breaks me.

"Forget what?"

"That you matter. That you're not expendable. That you're—" My voice catches. "That you're everything."

Something shifts in his expression—surprise giving way to something deeper. Something that looks like relief.

"Bree..."

But I'm already stepping back, my heart full and aching all at once. The moment feels complete somehow, like a promise I needed to make before everything changes.

"Come on," I say, turning toward the house. "We should probably start breakfast before the others wake up."

Jace follows, his footsteps quiet on the grass behind me. When I reach the door, I feel his fingers brush mine—tentative, hopeful. I don't pull away. Instead, I lace our fingers together, and his breath catches like he can't quite believe I'm letting him.

The mist trails behind us, peaceful now. Content.

Some bonds don't come from blood or magic or scars. Some are quieter than that. But no less real.

And sometimes the only way to say it is with a kiss you don't expect—

—and don't want to live without.

Chapter 18
JACE

She kissed me.

The thought loops through my head on a constant reel, like background music set to *yes please* on repeat.

Bree kissed me.

Not some in-the-heat, barely-thinking kiss—but slow. Certain. Chosen.

I'm walking six inches off the ground as we step back inside. Her hand's still in mine, and I have no plans of letting go. Ever.

The kitchen's dark except for the soft spill of early light from the windows, and for the first time in what feels like days, there's room to breathe.

"You, uh…" I clear my throat, trying to keep my voice level. "You hungry? Because I feel like I should feed you after that. Or maybe myself. Definitely both of us."

She laughs—*actually* laughs—and it's like somebody just cracked the sun in half and poured it straight into my chest.

"Are you saying kissing me was exhausting?" she teases, one brow raised.

"Oh, it was *life-changing,* sweetheart," I say, already scanning the pantry. "Which is why we need pancakes. Big, sugary, holy-shit-we're-alive pancakes."

Her lips part like she might argue, but then—she smiles. Soft and a little stunned.

"Holy shit we're alive pancakes?" she echoes, like she's trying the phrase on.

"The best kind," I confirm. "Fluffy and unnecessary and completely worth it."

I start pulling ingredients—flour, eggs, Rhett's secret vanilla stash—and Bree moves to the counter, watching with something like fond amusement as I attempt my one true domestic skill with one hand. Because again: *not letting go.*

She doesn't stop me. Doesn't tease. Just... leans, warm and *here*, her eyes brighter than they were when we left the backyard.

I could live in this moment forever.

Footsteps creak on the stairs. I glance up as Wes walks in, hair a mess, hoodie swallowing his whole frame.

"Morning," he says, blinking like he's still trying to decide if we're real.

"Couldn't sleep," Bree says easily.

"So," I add, flipping the first pancake, "we're making holy-shit-we're-alive pancakes."

Wes raises an eyebrow. "Is that a formal breakfast category now?"

"The most important one," I say, mock-serious. "Perfect for post-revelation, pre-sanctuary survival prep."

Gray's next, silent and observant, followed by Rhett and Theo. One by one, they fill the kitchen like puzzle pieces falling into place. Bree straightens a little under their gaze, but she doesn't move away from me.

Theo's the one who notices first. His gaze shifts—me, Bree, our joined hands, back to Bree's face—and he tilts his head, saying nothing.

Wes watches Bree for a beat too long. "Something's different," he says slowly. "Did we miss a moment?"

"Nope," I say, too fast.

"Definitely feels like a moment," Rhett murmurs.

Bree makes the smallest noise—somewhere between a laugh and a threat—and reaches for the coffee instead of defending herself.

I grin, unable to help it. "What can I say? I never kiss and tell."

The room *freezes* for half a second.

Then Bree flushes scarlet. Full-body embarrassment. And that alone might be the most beautiful thing I've ever seen.

She doesn't deny it. Doesn't deflect. Just sips her coffee with extreme focus while the others collectively *think very hard*.

No teasing. No jokes. Just... awareness.

And then the final beat lands.

The floor creaks. Two shadows emerge from the living room—Stellan, moving like liquid silk, and Thane, grumpy and rumpled in a way that makes it very obvious they slept on couches not meant for sleeping. Or someone his size.

They pause at the edge of the kitchen, and for a breath, everything stills.

Stellan's gaze lands on Bree first, then flicks to me. His expression doesn't change, but something in his posture does. Like he just walked into a spell already cast.

Thane squints like he smells emotional intimacy and would like it to leave immediately.

"Morning," I offer, pretending this isn't wildly awkward.

Stellan nods. "Something smells divine."

Thane's gaze settles on Bree, and there's something assessing in it. "Long journey ahead," he says. "What comes after... will be an adjustment."

Bree looks up from her coffee, meeting his eyes directly. Her voice is quiet but steady. "I'm stronger than I look."

The mist beneath the table stills, then sways toward her.

Stellan's mouth curves slightly—barely there, but definitely approving.

And all I can think is: *Damn right she is.*

Bree mumbles something about pancakes and coffee. Her hand is still in mine. She doesn't let go.

And I swear—for just a second—the mist curling beneath the table shifts like it's listening.

Like it *approves*.

"Better grab a plate," I say, flipping another round. "We're feeding the people we love before we go tear the world apart."

Rhett hums. "That's one way to start the day."

I glance at Bree. Her hair's a little windblown. Her cheeks are still flushed. There's pancake batter on my wrist and joy in my ribs and the girl I've loved since before I knew what love was just kissed me like she meant it.

Yeah. Holy-shit-we're-alive pancakes.

I pile them high.

Because if we're stepping into the unknown—if everything changes today—then this moment, right here, is how we begin:

Together.

Fed.

And finally, finally awake.

Chapter 19
THANE

The silence after breakfast sits heavy between us. I keep my hands steady on the wheel, eyes fixed on the road ahead, but my mind keeps circling back to the kitchen. To her. To the way she moved through that space like she belonged there—not tentative or grateful, but certain. Like she'd always been part of their rhythm.

The guys. Changed. All of them.

I could see it in the way Rhett's hands radiated heat when he reached for the coffee pot. In how the air shifted around Jace when he laughed. In the careful way Wes positioned himself near her, like he was drawn by invisible threads.

And her—standing in the middle of it all, fingers laced with Langston's, mist curling contentedly around her feet like it had found exactly where it wanted to be.

She's not what I expected.

Stellan hasn't spoken since we left the driveway. He sits in the passenger seat, impossibly relaxed, watching the landscape roll past with that infuriating calm of his. Like he's not bothered by any of this. Like watching five men awaken to powers they don't understand is just another Tuesday.

The silence stretches until it becomes a weight.

"You've been quiet," Stellan finally says.

I don't look at him. "I drive better when I'm not dissecting domestic affairs."

His mouth curves—I catch it in my peripheral vision. "Domestic affairs."

"Whatever you want to call it."

"I'd call it inevitable." He shifts in his seat, angling toward me. "The Ether has already changed them. It's not just magic, Thane. It's identity. Their bodies are beginning to respond to her presence."

"I know what I saw."

"Do you?" There's something sharp in his tone now. "Because what I saw was five men discovering they've been incomplete their entire lives. And one girl finally understanding just a hint of what she's capable of."

My grip tightens on the steering wheel. "She's untrained. Dangerous."

"To who?"

The question hangs between us, heavier than it should be. Because the answer isn't *to the world* or *to the magical balance* or any of the things I told the Council.

The answer is *to me*.

To everything I thought I understood about power and control. About being needed, but never wanted. About surviving in a world that sees Feeders like me—like Wes, like Stellan—as expendable.

But she didn't look at us like that.

Not once.

"The sanctuary will help," I say instead. "Structure. Boundaries. Training."

"Will it?"

I finally glance at him. "What's that supposed to mean?"

Stellan's watching me with that unsettling directness of his. "I mean, are you taking her there because you think she needs the structure? Or because you need the distance?"

I don't answer. Can't answer.

Because he's not wrong.

The miles pass in silence. The road ahead is straight and empty, cutting through farmland that gives way to forest as we near the sanctuary. I should be thinking about defenses, about the other Council members who might be watching, about the possibility that Bree has enemies we haven't identified yet.

Instead, I keep thinking about the way she looked at me this morning. Not afraid. Not grateful. Just... assessing. Like she was trying to figure out if I was worth her time.

She's not what I was told.

"You're unsettled," Stellan observes.

I don't reply.

The silence stretches again, broken only by the hum of tires on asphalt and the distant sound of wind through trees.

And then, out of nowhere:

"Damn. Those really were good pancakes."

Stellan's quiet laughter fills the car. He doesn't push, doesn't comment. Just lets the admission hang there like the confession it is.

Because it's not about the pancakes. It's about watching her move through their kitchen like she'd always belonged there. It's about the way Langston looked at her—like she'd handed him the sun. It's about how natural it all felt, even to me.

Especially to me.

"She's not what you expected," Stellan says quietly.

"No." The word comes out rougher than I intended. "She's worse."

He waits.

"She's real," I finish.

Not a weapon to be wielded or a threat to be contained. Not a political chess piece or a source of power to be claimed.

Just a girl who makes pancakes with her chosen family and kisses boys in gardens at dawn and carries mist like breathing.

A girl who's already changing everything, whether she means to or not.

The sanctuary boundary appears ahead—ancient stone markers barely visible through the trees. I should feel relief. We're almost there. Almost safe within walls that have protected the Scarborne line for centuries.

Instead, my chest feels tight.

That's when the mist appears.

A single thread of it, silver-green and gold, gliding across the hood of the car. From nowhere. No source, no reason.

I slam on the brakes.

The BMW skids to a stop, and a second later, brakes screech behind us. I glance in the rearview—Jace's car veering onto the shoulder, the others stacked behind, doors already opening.

They saw it too.

Or at least, they felt it

But the mist is still there, pooling now around the base of the stone markers like it's marking territory.

"She hasn't even stepped on the land yet," Stellan murmurs. "And already, it answers her."

He glances toward the forest beyond the stones, then back to me. "They'll come, you know."

I frown. "Who?"

He doesn't smile. Doesn't blink.

"The ones who remember what this place was. What it meant."

He looks at the mist pooling like it's waiting for someone. "The ones who still feel the pull."

I can't speak. Can't breathe.

She hasn't even stepped on the land yet.

And it's already hers.

And somehow, I think they'll know.

Chapter 20
BREE

The radio plays something soft between us, filling the space where conversation should be. Jace's fingers tap against the wheel, but the rhythm's off—like he's distracted. Like we both are. The kiss still lingers between us, unspoken but loud in the quiet.

I watch the landscape blur past—fields giving way to trees, farmland dissolving into something wilder. The mist curls against my ankles, restless but not urgent. Waiting.

Something in my chest tightens. Not fear. Something else.

"You're quiet," Jace says, glancing at me sideways. His green eyes catch the morning light, concern threading through the gold flecks I've always loved.

"Just watching," I say, because *thinking* feels too complicated for what's happening inside me.

Jace's fingers still on the wheel. "Bree—"

That's when Thane's BMW slams on the brakes ahead of us.

The sudden stop makes my breath catch, but not from the jolt. From something else. Something that pulls at the space beneath my sternum before I even see what made him stop. His car skids slightly as it veers onto the shoulder, gravel spraying beneath his tires.

"What the hell?" Jace mutters, following suit. Our car rocks slightly as we come to a stop behind Thane's shimmering green BMW—a color that reminds me of something I can't quite place, something that makes my chest tight with recognition.

Through Thane's rear window, I can see his silhouette. Unnaturally still. Staring ahead at something I can't see from here.

My hand is already on the door handle before I realize I'm moving.

"Bree, wait—"

But I can't wait. Something pulls at me like gravity, like recognition.

My feet hit the gravel, and the mist immediately swirls higher, expectant. Behind me, car doors slam—Jace's voice rising, the others close behind. But they sound muffled, distant. Like I'm hearing them through water.

I approach Thane's driver's side window. He turns toward me, and for a second, his careful mask slips completely. There's something raw in his silver eyes. Something shaken and wondering.

"You okay?" I ask.

"The road decided to surprise me," he says, but his voice carries an edge I've never heard before. Uncertainty. Maybe even awe.

I follow his gaze toward the trees.

At first, I see nothing. Just forest. Just ordinary shadows between ordinary trunks.

And then somehow, I'm walking.

No decision. No thought. Just movement—quiet and inevitable—as if my body knows something my mind doesn't.

The mist around me rises to meet it, calm and sure.

I don't look back.

My feet just carry me forward, slow and instinctive, like I'm moving through a dream. Behind me, voices rise—Jace's footsteps starting after me, then stopping. Others call my name. But they're distant now, behind the trees and the moment.

The tree line approaches. Each step makes my heart pound harder, but not from fear. It's anticipation coursing through me.

What if this isn't meant for me? What if I'm wrong about everything?

But the mist curls around my ankles like encouragement, and I keep walking.

One step. Another.

And then I cross some invisible threshold, and everything changes.

The mist bursts around me like living starlight—silver, shimmering in air that suddenly tastes different. Sweet. Electric. Alive. The light shifts, breaking through the canopy where shadows had been thick before. A soft breeze stirs the leaves, and they lean toward me, just slightly. Just enough to make my breath catch.

Something that feels like coming home.

The thought stops me cold. Not because I understand it—because I *feel* it.

The path ahead begins to clear, overgrowth seeming to pull back without sound or signal. Flowers bloom in my peripheral vision, tiny bursts of color where there should be shadow. Small animals emerge from hiding—a rabbit, a cardinal, something that might be a fox—all watching with bright, curious eyes. Not afraid.

Almost... welcoming.

The mist winds around my ankles like silk, tender and expectant. Each step feels like a conversation I don't have words for yet.

I keep walking, almost afraid to breathe too loudly. Afraid to break whatever spell has settled over this place. The trees seem to whisper secrets I can almost hear, their voices threading together into something that might be my name.

The forest feels like I've stepped through a doorway into somewhere time moves differently.

I almost miss it.

I'm so focused on the way the light dances between the leaves that I nearly walk past the clearing entirely. Only the shift in sound stops me—the whispers going quiet, like the forest is holding its breath.

I turn, and there it is.

An old stone well, nearly hidden by vines that seem to part like curtains as I approach. The air around it hums with something sacred, something patient. The kind of quiet that holds space for wishes and secrets and prayers spoken into dark water.

The mist pools around the well's base, glowing faintly against the moss-covered stones. Like it's been waiting here for me to find it.

A wishing well. I was raised on stories about wishing wells, about dropping coins into dark water and hoping for magic. But when I check my pockets, I find nothing except lint and the weight of wanting things I can't bring myself to think about.

I'm about to turn away when something catches the light.

A coin, lying on the mossy ground as if it had just fallen there. But it doesn't look dropped. It looks placed. Deliberately. For me.

I kneel, and the moment my fingers close around it, warmth spreads up my arm.

The coin is unlike anything I've ever seen—ancient, iridescent, alive with possibility.

It doesn't look forged. It looks born. Like it grew from the earth itself, waiting for this moment.

I close my hand around it. Hold it there for a beat. Let the weight of it settle.

What could I even wish for?

I could wish for safety. For the fear to stop. For answers that make sense. For the guys behind me to stop looking at me like I'm something precious they might break.

But I don't want safety. I don't want to go back.

I want to understand. I want to be worthy of whatever trust this place is showing me. I want to stop running from whatever I'm becoming and run toward it instead.

The wish forms not in words but in feeling—a deep, aching hope that I can be what this land thinks I am. What the mist believes I can become. What the guys see when they look at me like I'm not broken beyond repair.

I don't say it aloud. Some wishes are too big for words, too fragile for air. But I make it anyway, holding the coin tight against my chest before dropping it into the well's dark mouth.

It falls without a sound.

The moment stretches, suspended. Even the wind stops breathing. The forest holds its breath.

Then the mist curls upward, just once, like a nod. Like acceptance.

Like the wish was heard.

I turn, finally remembering I'm not alone, and find them all standing at the edge of the trees.

Five figures watching in silence, caught between shadow and sunlight.

Even Thane looks shaken, his usual composure cracked enough to show something raw underneath.

Stellan stands apart, unreadable as always, but his gaze is steady. Focused entirely on me—like he's seeing something he expected but wasn't ready to face.

The mist drifts between the trunks behind me, curling upward like a quiet invitation.

I don't feel distant from them. Just... shifted.

Like something old and quiet has seen me, and I don't quite fit where I stood before.

I take one more step toward the deeper forest.

The trees adjust, letting light spill through in narrow beams. The path behind me glows faintly, like memory, like breath.

And in the hush that follows, I don't hear words.

Just a feeling.

Something familiar.

Maybe I wasn't just meant to find this place.

Maybe it's been waiting to find me, too

Chapter 21
RHETT

She turns back toward us, and I forget how to breathe.

The mist pools around her feet like liquid starlight, and the path she just walked shimmers faintly—like the forest is still glowing from her touch somehow. Her hair catches the filtered light, dark waves framing a face I've memorized a thousand times—but somehow, it looks different now. Changed.

God, she's never looked more beautiful.

And then reality crashes back in like cold water.

What the hell was she thinking, just walking away like that? No explanation, no warning, just... gone. Into a forest we don't know, toward something we can't see, while we stood there like idiots watching her disappear.

My hands clench at my sides, heat building beneath my skin. The familiar spiral starts—fear masquerading as anger, protectiveness trying to translate itself into control. She could have been hurt. She could have gotten lost. She could have—

A crow caws overhead.

Sharp. Deliberate. Off.

I look up automatically, tracking the sound to a thick branch maybe thirty feet away. Black wings shift, settle. Dark eyes that seem too intelligent. Too focused.

It's watching us. Watching *her*.

That's when I notice Thane.

He's stepped forward, silver eyes following my line of sight, head tilted at an angle that makes my spine prickle. Every line of his body has gone tense, alert—like he's listening to something the rest of us can't hear.

The bird shifts again, and instinct kicks in hard and fast.

We're being watched. Something's off. And then it hits me like a sledgehammer to the chest.

"Shit—the cars."

The words explode out of me before I can think. Jace whips around, green eyes wide.

"Wait, what?"

"Oh my god." Theo's voice cracks slightly. "We left them *running*."

Stellan's voice cuts through the sudden chaos, flat and amused. "Keys are still in the ignition."

And then we're moving.

Jace takes off first, already laughing—that manic, breathless sound he makes when panic and relief crash into each other. "I'm gonna marry that car if it survived this," he wheezes, dodging low branches.

Theo's right behind him, muttering to himself in that way he does when he's trying to process something his brain can't quite catalogue. "It felt like the trees moved. And there was a fox. Or something fox-adjacent. Do foxes normally—"

"Theo, run now, wildlife inventory later," I call out, pushing past him.

Wes follows last, not rushing, like this is all mildly entertaining rather than potentially catastrophic. "I'm not saying I'd kill someone over that jacket," he murmurs. "I'm just saying I wouldn't *not*."

Gray half-runs, half-laughs beside me. "We leave running vehicles unattended next to magical forests now? Cool. That's our thing?"

The sound of our engines grows louder as we get closer, and relief floods through me so hard my knees almost buckle. Still running. Still there. Still *ours*.

We burst into the clearing where we left them, and it's like stumbling back into the normal world. Three cars, exactly where we left them, engines purring contentedly in the afternoon air.

I go straight to my truck, yanking open the driver's door. Keys dangling from the ignition, doors unlocked—everything exactly as we abandoned it in our rush to follow her into whatever was calling.

Jace reaches his car and actually pats the roof like it's a living thing. "Good boy. Who's a good car? *You* are. Yes, you are."

"You're embarrassing," Wes observes, but there's fondness in it.

Gray's already doing perimeter—checking doors, mirrors, anything that might be wrong. Methodical. Steady. It's what he does when the world stops making sense—impose order wherever he can find it.

Theo slows down, no longer worried about the car. He's processing something bigger; I can see it in the way his shoulders haven't relaxed, the way his eyes keep drifting back toward the forest.

"It's not just her," he says quietly. "The forest—it's doing things."

I look at him, not dismissive but not ready to dive headfirst into whatever magical theory he's building either. "What kind of things?"

Theo's eyes track the tree line again. "Like it knows us," he says. "Like it's been waiting."

He goes quiet, breathing a little too hard. His gaze flicks between us like he's hoping someone else will say it first.

Then he half-laughs—nervous, a little breathless.

"That's weird, right? Like... forests don't usually do that?"

Jace doesn't miss a beat. "Cool. Great. Love that. Everyone still in their original bodies? Fantastic."

I don't answer. I'm too busy wondering if the forest really *has* been waiting—and what the hell it's waiting for.

Wes is already near the car when he stops short. Opens the back door.

He stares at something inside, just long enough for me to notice.

"Did one of you move my jacket?" he asks, voice low. Not angry. Just... off.

Gray looks up from the passenger side. "Nope."

Wes doesn't say anything else. He just smooths the fabric back into place like that'll make it better.

He might've joked on the way back to the cars, but he's not joking now.

I round the front of my truck, trying to shake it off—and that's when I see it.

A feather.

Caught behind the grill. Small. Black. *Wrong.*

I pull it free. Glossy. Sharp at the tip.

How did this get here?

When I glance up, Wes is already watching me.

Gray catches the look between us. Doesn't say a word. Just keeps moving—but slower now. More careful.

I toss the feather aside before I can decide if I'm just being paranoid.

But the tension doesn't lift.

The adrenaline's fading now, leaving behind the crash that always follows. I lean against my truck and take inventory, the way I always do when the world tilts sideways.

Jace is still vibrating, laughing too hard at nothing. Theo hasn't spoken in thirty seconds, which might be a personal record. Wes looks like a statue—arms crossed, unreadable, processing whatever just happened in that quiet way of his. And Gray's still moving, still circling, like the forest might suddenly grow teeth.

Everyone's unraveling in their own way.

I just happen to do it quietly.

"We should go," I say finally. Because standing here won't change what we just saw, won't make it make sense, won't bring her back from whatever she found in that clearing.

Jace sighs and tosses his keys at Gray without looking. "You drive. I'm spiritually unwell."

Gray catches them one-handed. "So unwell you're driving Thane's BMW?"

Jace smirks as he folds himself into the car

One by one, we pile back into our vehicles. The mood shifts, quiets, like the laughter was just a pressure valve and now we're all settling into the weight of what comes next.

I grip the wheel tighter than I need to, checking my mirrors one more time before putting the truck in drive. I can see the BMW already moving, leading us deeper into whatever this day is becoming.

We fall in behind it, engines purring like we haven't just stepped into something unknown.

But all I can hear is her name.

And the way the forest answered it.

Chapter 22
BREE

The crow calls again, sharp and deliberate, cutting through the sacred quiet that still clings to the clearing. I'm standing at the edge of where normal forest becomes something else—where the path I walked still shimmers faintly with residual light.

Behind me, I can hear the others regrouping. Voices carrying across the distance, footsteps on gravel, the sound of car doors slamming. They found their way back to the cars. Good. I hadn't even thought about that until now, but the relief settles warm in my chest anyway.

The crow calls a third time, and something about it makes my skin crawl. It's not just the sound—it's the timing. The way it feels deliberate. Like it's trying to get someone's attention.

Soft footsteps approach from behind. Not rushing, but there's tension in them.

"That's not just a crow." Thane's voice carries an edge I haven't heard before.

I turn to look at him, then follow his gaze up to the tree. The bird sits perfectly still now, watching us with those too-intelligent eyes.

"What do you mean?"

"Shifter." His jaw ticks. "Council representative. Nyx." The name comes out like a curse. "She's... observing."

"Spying, you mean."

His mouth quirks, just barely. "Observing."

The wrongness I felt crystallizes into something colder. "Someone's watching us."

"Yes." His silver eyes are hard now, angry. "And she's not supposed to be here."

The crow shifts on its branch, and something about the movement makes my skin crawl. Like it's listening to every word, cataloguing every detail to report back.

"She won't leave," I say.

"No. Not unless you make her."

I frown, looking between him and the bird. "How?"

"Use your Ether."

The word hits different than 'mist.' Heavier. More real. "The mist?"

"The Ether," he corrects, and something in his tone makes it clear this distinction matters. "That's what it's called. What you are."

I stare up at the crow, then back at him. "How?"

"The same way you opened the path. The same way the forest answered you." His silver eyes study my face. "Set a boundary. Make it clear she's not welcome."

I close my eyes, trying to feel for that same instinct that guided me to the well. The mist—the Ether—stirs around my ankles, but when I reach for it, it slips away like trying to hold water.

"I don't—"

"Don't think. Feel."

I try again, this time focusing on the feeling rather than the how. The sense of wrongness, of being watched by something that doesn't belong.

The Ether responds, rising around me like a protective barrier, and I push that feeling outward.

Not welcome. Not here. Go.

The crow launches off the branch so suddenly I jump, black wings beating hard against the air as it disappears into the deeper forest.

My knees nearly buckle with the effort, but satisfaction floods through me anyway. I did that. I made it leave.

Thane steps forward instinctively—like he's going to steady me—but stops short. Hands hovering. Watching me.

"Why do you only let Jace touch you?"

The question catches me off guard.

I straighten slowly, bracing myself without help. "I don't."

He doesn't respond right away. Just studies me with that too-perceptive gaze, like he's trying to measure something invisible.

"I saw him holding your hand earlier," he says quietly. "At breakfast. The others hold back."

"It's complicated," I mutter.

He hums, low and unreadable. "Is it trust?"

I glance away, suddenly needing the forest more than the conversation. "It's survival."

A beat of silence.

Then, softer: "For what it's worth... I understand what it means to be touched less."

That stops me. Not fully, but enough to hear the edge under his voice.

We walk in silence for a while, the Ether curling lazily around my ankles again—like it's watching both of us now.

"So what happened to me back there?" I ask finally. "At the well.

"I don't fully know," he says, and I can tell he's choosing his words carefully. Not lying, but not telling me everything either.

I file that away for later and try a different approach.

"You told all of the guys what they were. What are you?"

He's quiet for so long I think he might not answer. Then: "A Feeder."

"And that's...?"

His jaw ticks, just slightly. "Nothing you need to worry about."

The dismissal in his tone makes something hot and sharp rise in my chest. "I know what it feels like to be treated like I'm less," I say, stopping abruptly. "I won't do that to someone else. So try again."

He turns to face me fully, silver eyes searching my expression like he's trying to solve a puzzle. After a long moment, he exhales.

"Feeders survive off energy. Magic, emotion, life force—it depends on the individual. We're not..." He pauses, choosing his words. "We're not always respected. Some see us as parasitic. Dangerous. Necessary, but barely tolerated."

The words land like stones in my stomach. "That's why they don't respect you."

"Yes."

"That's why they sent you."

"Yes."

I study his face—the careful mask, the controlled expression that doesn't quite hide the years of dealing with being seen as less than. "And yet... you volunteered."

"I did."

"Why?"

His mouth curves into something that might be a smile if it reached his eyes. "Just like I told you—I thought you were going to be a problem."

I cross my arms, not buying it. "And why did you really volunteer?"

This time his expression shifts, becomes something more honest. "Because I needed to see you for myself."

I don't answer him. Just start walking again, faster this time, the Ether swirling around my feet like it's annoyed on my behalf.

Behind us, maybe ten paces back, I can hear Stellan following. Not trying to catch up, not trying to disappear either. Just... there. When I glance back, he's watching with that unreadable expression of his, like he knows exactly what conversation just happened and finds it mildly entertaining.

"The hierarchy," I say after another stretch of silence. "It's based on power?"

"Perception of power," Thane corrects. "Elementals and Shifters are seen as pure magic. Seers are respected for their gifts. Mentalists..." His lip curls slightly. "Mentalists think they're superior to everyone."

He pauses, studying my face. "And then there are Sources."

"Sources?"

"The original magic. Bloodlines that can create bonds, amplify others' power, channel raw magic." His voice goes quiet. "They used to rule everything. Until most were hunted down."

Something cold settles in my stomach. "Most?"

"There are other Source bloodlines left, but they're far less powerful. They've been left alone." He stops walking entirely. "Your bloodline—the Scarborne line—was the only one that wielded Ether. And that died out generations ago. You're the first Scarborne to manifest Ether in over a century. That's why the Council is afraid. That's why they sent me. Ether doesn't just reshape magic—it reshapes everything."

I stare at him, trying to process what he's saying. "And Feeders?"

"Are at the bottom," he finishes. "Always."

The injustice of it burns in my chest. "That's bullshit."

He glances at me sideways. "Perhaps. But it's the way things are."

"It doesn't have to be."

"No," he says quietly. "I suppose it doesn't."

The forest around us is changing as we walk—less wild, more structured. Like we're approaching something built rather than grown. The sanctuary, maybe. Whatever that means.

"They're afraid of you," I realize suddenly. "That's why they sent you instead of coming themselves. They're afraid of what I might do."

"Yes."

"But you're not."

He stops walking, and when I turn to face him, there's something raw in his expression. Something that looks almost like surprise.

"No," he says finally. "I'm not."

The admission hangs between us, weighted with everything he's not saying. Behind us, Stellan has stopped too, still watching, still silent.

"Good," I say, echoing his earlier approval. "Because I'm tired of being afraid."

The Ether pulses once around my ankles, like agreement. Like a promise.

And when we start walking again, it feels less like following a path and more like forging one.

Chapter 23
WES

Through the windshield, I watch three figures walk down from the upper path like they've found their own way here. Bree moves between Thane and Stellan, and even from this distance, there's something different about her—something that makes the hunger in my chest twist tighter, sharper than it's been all day.

Rhett's hands are steady on the wheel, but I can feel the tension radiating off him in waves. The silence in the truck feels thick enough to choke on. In the car ahead, Gray drives while Theo sits passenger, both of them focused on the approaching group with that careful attention that means everyone's trying not to fall apart.

I press my fingers into the leather seat, trying to keep myself anchored. The hunger isn't pain anymore—it's an absence that's been growing louder with every breath, like a frequency I can't quite tune out but can't ignore either.

"You hanging in there?" Rhett asks, catching my eye in the rearview mirror.

"Always."

The lie tastes familiar by now. We both know it's bullshit, but Rhett just nods and doesn't push. I'm grateful for that—for the space he gives me to fall apart quietly.

The cars park side by side at the base of the hill. Ahead of us, a path cuts through the overgrowth toward what must be the sanctuary's threshold, and the air here feels different. Older. Like the land itself has been holding its breath for centuries, waiting for her to come home.

Bree looks radiant—there's no other word for it. She stands between Thane and Stellan like she's finally found her place in the world, the Ether curling around her ankles with something that looks almost like contentment.

The guys step out of their cars—Jace from the BMW he drove alone, Gray and Theo from Jace's car. Doors slam in the afternoon quiet, but I hang back, one hand still on the doorframe. Everything feels too bright—like the light's pressing in where my skin's already too tight.

Gray notices. Of course he does. He always notices the things the rest of us try to hide.

"Hey," he says, voice pitched low enough that the others can't hear. "Come here a sec."

He doesn't wait for me to argue, just starts walking toward the tree line where the sounds of the group will fade into something manageable. I follow because I don't know what else to do, and because the alternative is standing here pretending I'm fine while everyone watches me fail at it.

We find a spot where the undergrowth is soft and the afternoon light filters through leaves in patterns that should feel peaceful. Instead, it just makes me more restless, like even the forest knows something's wrong with me.

Gray turns to face me, hands in his pockets, expression careful in that way that means he's already figured out more than I want him to.

"You're not okay."

"Is anyone?" I ask, aiming for humor and missing by miles.

"You didn't touch your food this morning. Didn't speak on the drive. You look like you're about to bolt." His gray eyes study my face with that quiet intensity that sees everything I'm trying to hide. "You're starving."

The word hits too close to real, and suddenly I can't keep the words inside anymore. They tear out of me, raw and sharp and more honest than I intended.

"It's not just hunger. It's shame." I run a hand through my hair, hating how my voice cracks. "I don't want to want this. I don't want to be the guy who feeds off the people he cares about."

Gray steps closer, and I tense, expecting him to back away now that I've said it out loud. Because he knows what I am. Instead, his hand settles on my shoulder—warm and anchoring and completely unafraid.

"Then don't take," he says simply. "Just... feel. Try. You won't hurt me."

"Gray—"

"Trust me."

I close my eyes, hating how much I want to believe him. The Ether hums around us—not Bree's, but something else, something that feels like it's been sleeping inside me for years, waiting for permission to wake up.

I don't touch him. Just focus on the space between us, on the warmth radiating from his skin, on the steady rhythm of his breathing. Try to feel for whatever Stellan was talking about, that thread he said existed.

Nothing.

I try again, reaching for something I don't understand, and there's still nothing. Just the same gnawing absence that's been eating at me for too long.

"I can't—" I start to pull back, to brush this off like it was a stupid idea.

But Gray's hand tightens on my shoulder. "Don't give up yet."

He steps closer, close enough that I can feel the heat radiating off his skin. Close enough that when I breathe in, I catch the scent of cedar and something that's purely him.

And then—there.

Just a sip. A taste of something warm and wanting that definitely isn't mine.

The hunger responds like I've touched a live wire. Instead of easing, it amplifies, compounds, creates this feedback loop that makes my knees buckle. Gray's desire hits me in waves—not just attraction, but something deeper, hungrier, more raw than I expected.

"What—" I gasp, eyes flying open.

Gray's pupils are blown wide, his breathing as ragged as mine. "I don't know," he says, voice rough. "But I don't want it to stop."

Neither do I.

His mouth finds mine before I can think, hot and desperate and tasting like coffee and want. I pull him closer, fisting my hands in his shirt, and he responds by pushing me back against the nearest tree. The rough bark bites into my spine, but I don't care. The scent of cedar and sweat fills my lungs.

I can't tell where my hunger ends and his begins. Every breath feeds the loop between us, makes it stronger, more desperate. His teeth graze my bottom lip and I gasp, the sound swallowed by his mouth. My hands find his hair, soft and thick between my fingers, and when I tug, the noise he makes goes straight through me.

The world narrows to this—his weight against me, the taste of him on my tongue, the way his heart pounds under my palm when I spread my hand across his chest. Heat pools low in my stomach, sharp and demanding, and I'm drowning in want that might be his, might be mine, might be both of us spiraling together.

When we finally break apart, I can barely breathe. My lips feel swollen, my skin too tight. Gray's forehead rests against mine, both of us shaking.

"Shit," I whisper, the word barely more than breath.

"Yeah," he agrees, voice wrecked. "That was..."

He doesn't finish. Can't finish. Neither can I.

"Shit." I take a step back, running shaking hands through my hair. "I'm sorry, I—"

"You didn't hurt me," Gray says quietly, and there's something in his voice that makes me look up.

"I wanted to."

"Yeah." A pause, and then his mouth curves into something that might be a smile. "Me too."

The admission hangs between us, weighted with everything we're not saying. I feel calmer now—still starving, but centered in a way I haven't been in weeks. Like I've finally found something that fits, something that makes sense of all the pieces of myself I've been trying to hide.

We walk back toward the group in silence, my shirt wrinkled and Gray's hair a disaster, neither of us bothering to pretend otherwise.

Stellan is waiting for us, leaning against a tree with his arms crossed and that knowing expression that suggests he's been watching the whole time.

"Well," he says, dry as dust. "That didn't take long."

Jace stares openly, his green eyes wide with something between surprise and approval. Rhett pretends not to notice, but his shoulders are tense with the effort of not looking. Theo blinks like he did notice but is already filing it away for later analysis.

I should feel embarrassed. Exposed. Instead, I just feel wanted—genuinely, completely wanted for exactly what I am. It's a feeling I could get addicted to.

Bree steps forward, and for just a moment, something flickers across her face—something that looks almost like longing before she covers it with a smile that doesn't quite reach her eyes.

"Ready?" she asks, and something in her voice makes the Ether around her pulse brighter, more alive.

I nod, Gray's warmth still echoing through that thread between us, and follow her toward whatever's waiting at the sanctuary gate.

Chapter 24
BREE

The hill is steeper than it looked from the road.

My legs burn by the time we reach the top, and I'm trying not to breathe too hard because Thane and Stellan don't even look winded. Of course they don't. I bet they could climb mountains without breaking a sweat.

But when I see the ruins, breathing becomes the least of my problems.

"Oh," I whisper.

It's not what I expected. Not some crumbling pile of rocks or tourist-trap ancient monument. It's... broken, yes. But broken beautiful. Like someone took something magnificent and scattered the pieces just deliberately enough that you can still see what it used to be.

Arches that frame empty air. Walls that stop mid-sentence. Ivy threading through carved stone like it's trying to hold everything together with green fingers.

The mist around my ankles shifts, and for a second I swear it feels... eager.

"Where are the crews?" Thane's voice cuts through whatever moment I was having.

I look at him. He's scanning the ruins like he's reading a report that doesn't match the data. Expecting noise, maybe. People working.

Instead, there's just quiet.

A man emerges from behind a half-collapsed wall, dust coating his work clothes. He looks tired in a way that goes deeper than a long day. More like a long month of days that didn't go right.

When he sees Thane, his shoulders sag with relief.

"Finally," he says. "Thought you weren't coming back."

Thane's expression tightens. "Progress report?"

The man laughs, but there's no humor in it. "Progress. Sure." He waves a hand at the ruins. "We try every day. Doesn't stick. Every night it goes back."

"Goes back?" Stellan asks, like he's only mildly curious.

"Stones we move end up where we found them. Walls we shore up fall down again. Tools disappear, then show up exactly where we left them yesterday morning." The worker shakes his head. "Place has a memory, and it doesn't want us here."

Thane frowns like this is personally offensive to him. "That's not—"

But I'm not listening anymore. Something's pulling at me from deeper in the ruins. Not scary pulling. More like... like when you hear your name called from another room and you go to see who it was.

My feet start moving before I decide to walk.

"Bree." Thane's voice, sharp enough to cut.

I should stop. Should explain. Should do something other than wander off toward broken stone and empty spaces.

Instead, I keep walking.

The mist follows, but not like usual—no restless swirl. It knows where it's going.

There's an archway ahead—tall enough that I'd have to stretch to touch the top, carved with symbols that make my eyes water if I look too long.

The stone is pale, almost white, and somehow it feels warm even though the day isn't.

My hand reaches out. Just to touch. Just to see if it feels as warm as it looks.

The moment my fingers brush the stone, light blooms under my palm.

Not harsh. Not sudden. Just... there. Like someone lit a candle behind frosted glass. Silver lines trace patterns in the rock, and the mist around my legs moves toward them like it's been invited.

Something low hums through the stone, like a memory remembering itself.

"Bree?" Jace's voice, closer than I thought he was. "What's that?"

I don't know how to answer. Because I'm not doing anything. Not on purpose.

But the light is spreading anyway.

It seeps into cracks in the stone, follows the edges of broken tiles, pools in spaces where things should connect but don't. And wherever it goes, things start... settling.

Vines that were choking the archway loosen up, winding around the stone in patterns that actually look pretty instead of destructive. The cracked tiles under my feet do this little pulse—barely there, like a heartbeat—and suddenly they fit together again.

A path clears in front of me. Not like someone swept it clean, but like someone pulled back a curtain to show what was always there.

"Is she doing that?" Jace whispers.

"Looks like it," Wes says, and there's something in his voice I can't identify.

I take a step forward because the path is there and it feels rude not to use it. The stone glows softly where my foot touches, not like a spotlight but more like moonlight on water.

The others follow behind me. I can hear their footsteps, careful and quiet, but it feels like they're watching a movie and I'm the one inside it.

We walk into what must have been a garden once.

The trees are massive—older than anything I've ever seen, with bark that has silver veins running through it like lightning frozen mid-strike. Their leaves are purple, falling slow like they're underwater. Pretty in a way that makes my chest tight.

But what stops me cold isn't the trees.

It's the daisies.

They're scattered in clusters, white petals catching the light like glass. Just like the ones I planted back home. Only... more. Larger. Sharper. Their crystalline stems hum with that same soft chime—but louder now. Brighter. Like they've been waiting for me to find them again.

The sight hits me harder than it should. These impossible flowers that started as seeds by a door I couldn't open, that grew in my backyard and chimed like music. Now they're here, in this ancient place, blooming like they belong.

Like they've always belonged.

"Are those...?" Rhett's voice trails off.

"The ones from home," I whisper, because there's no mistaking them. The same perfect white petals, the same glass-like stems. But transformed. Elevated.

As I watch, more flowers bloom around them. Just like that. Buds opening into white and silver petals. Paths straightening into perfect lines. Garden beds clearing of weeds, organizing into neat rows.

It's beautiful.

It's also completely wrong.

I stop in the middle of it all, skin prickling with wrongness. It's too clean. Too organized. Like someone took a song and forced it into the wrong key.

"No," I say out loud, surprising myself. "That's not right."

The mist around me goes still, like it's waiting for instructions.

I think about how the garden looked when we walked in. Wild, sure. Overgrown, definitely. But alive in a way that felt honest. The ivy wasn't destroying the stones—it was holding them together. The scattered flowers weren't messy—they were scattered like someone had thrown confetti at a party.

Even the daisies looked better when they were growing wild, nestled among the weeds and broken stones like secrets.

I liked it better before.

The thought is barely finished when everything changes.

The neat lines soften. Petals spill out of their perfect arrangements, scattering across the ground in patterns that look random but feel right. The ivy creeps back, but gently this time. Like it's hugging instead of strangling.

The daisies settle back into their natural clusters, their crystalline stems chiming softly as they adjust. Content now. Home.

The garden breathes again.

"Did she just... undo a week of restoration by thinking about it?" Jace asks, and he sounds like he's trying not to laugh.

I turn around to look at them. Rhett looks stunned. Wes is watching me with that quiet intensity that makes my stomach flip. Theo's eyes are wide like he's seeing something that rewrites everything he thought he knew.

"I have no idea how I did that," I admit, because it's true.

That's when Thane makes a sound like someone punched him.

He's standing next to what was definitely a pile of rubble when we walked past it five minutes ago. Now there's a wall. A whole, complete, perfectly intact wall that looks like it was built yesterday.

"This wasn't here," he says, and his voice is strange. Shaky.

Stellan walks over and runs his hand along the new stone. For once, he's not smirking. "Of course it wasn't," he says quietly. "It wasn't meant for us."

I catch something in the way he says it. Like there's more to that sentence. "Meant for who?"

His gray eyes find mine. "For you."

The mist pulses once around my ankles, and I swear the stones around us are listening. Waiting. The daisies pulse brighter in response, their light echoing the rhythm of my heartbeat.

I start walking again because standing still feels wrong. The path curves between walls that definitely weren't there before, leading deeper into the ruins. With each step, the glow under my feet gets brighter, tracing patterns that feel familiar even though I've never seen them before.

Symbols appear on the doorways we pass. Simple ones at first, then more complicated. Spirals and geometric shapes that hurt to follow with your eyes. They should mean something. I feel like they should mean something.

And then we reach the big one.

It's massive—at least twice my height, carved from stone that gleams like polished silver. The frame is covered in symbols so intricate they seem to move when I'm not looking straight at them. The door itself is heavy wood banded with metal that looks like it hasn't been touched in years.

I walk toward it because that seems to be what I do now. Walk toward things that probably shouldn't be walked toward.

The moment I get close enough to touch it, the door shudders.

Not like someone pushed it. Like it just remembered what doors are supposed to do.

The wood groans—not with strain, but with recognition. The hinges protest for about half a second, then give up and let the door swing open. Smooth as anything.

Darkness beyond. But not empty darkness. Expectant darkness.

I take a step back, hands up like I'm surrendering. "I didn't touch it."

"No," Stellan says, and there's something almost like approval in his voice. "It opened for you."

I stare at the open doorway. At the darkness that doesn't feel threatening, just... waiting. Like a room waiting for someone it already knew.

The mist flows toward the threshold, drawn by whatever's in there.

I look back at the others. At Jace's wide eyes and Rhett's careful stillness. At Wes's quiet hunger and Theo's reverent expression. At Gray, who meets my gaze for just a second, unreadable. Quiet, like he's already felt something shift. And Thane, who looks like his entire understanding of the world just got rewritten.

Then I look at the waiting darkness.

And because I'm apparently the kind of person who walks through doors meant for someone else now, I do.

Chapter 25
THEO

I've seen this.

Not the room exactly, but this moment. Bree stepping forward into a silence that holds its breath. The Ether choosing. The way everything holds its breath before the world shifts on its axis.

But visions are supposed to warn you. Not fall into place like fate.

The sanctuary unfolds around us as we follow her through the threshold. I'm caught between two pulls—watching the architecture bloom to life around Bree's footsteps, and watching her face as she experiences it. Both steal my breath for different reasons.

The air is charged, thick with magic that clings to the walls like memory. The structure hums—not audibly, but something deeper. Like it knows it's being seen again after centuries of sleep.

Bree doesn't lead on purpose, but we follow her anyway. Like she's meant to be here. Like this place has been waiting for her specifically.

Rooms reveal themselves as she passes. Sigils carved into doorframes flicker to life when she's near, then fade to a gentle glow behind her. Furniture repositions itself without sound—a chair sliding into place, a table straightening, debris simply disappearing like it was never there. Light filters through arches that weren't there moments ago, casting everything in warm gold.

It's exactly as I've seen in dreams. Every detail, every turn of the corridor. But the fact that it's real scares me more than it should.

I steal glances at Bree as we walk. She's not afraid—there's wonder in her expression, quiet awe that makes something in my chest pull tight. The Ether flows around her ankles like a cat seeking attention, and she seems... settled. Like she's finally somewhere she belongs.

And gods, it *does* something to me—seeing her like that. Like maybe the wounds are knitting, even if just at the edges. Like maybe the girl who shook in her sleep is letting herself rest.

Behind me, Thane's controlled composure is cracking. His silver eyes dart from wall to wall, cataloging changes that don't make sense.

"This wasn't here last week," he whispers, voice rough with disbelief.

Stellan moves beside him with that predatory grace of his, but he's quieter than usual. Almost reverent. "She's not restoring it," he murmurs. "She's rewriting it."

The corridor opens into a circular atrium, and I have to stop walking. Because this—this is the heart of what I've been seeing in fragments. The curved walls, the way light pools in the center, the sense of something sacred and protected.

Bree pauses too, tilting her head like she's listening to something none of us can hear. The Ether rises higher around her legs, expectant.

That's when I see it.

A door that wasn't there before—tall and elegant, carved from pale wood that gleams like pearl. It stands opposite where we entered, and as we watch, silver lines trace across its surface in patterns that make my eyes water if I look too long.

"This is it," I breathe, not meaning to speak aloud.

Jace glances at me. "This is what?"

But I can't answer. Because the door is opening.

Not with a creak or groan. It swings inward, smooth as silk, revealing darkness beyond that somehow doesn't feel empty. Expectant darkness. Welcoming darkness.

Bree approaches slowly, the Ether pooling at her feet like it's gathering courage. When she reaches the threshold, she stops and looks back at us.

"You should see this," she says softly.

It's permission and invitation all at once.

I step forward first, drawn by the same instinct that's been guiding me since the visions started. The others follow, our footsteps muffled by something softer than stone.

And then we're inside.

This is what a dream feels like the moment before you wake—too perfect to exist, but undeniably real. The chamber spreads out in a perfect circle, vast enough that the far walls blur into gentle shadow. The ceiling arches high above us, smooth stone that holds its own warm light.

But it's not the size that steals my breath.

It's the bed.

It rises from the center of the room like an altar to comfort—low and wide and round, draped in fabrics that catch the light and hold it. Velvet in deep blues and silvers, linen that looks impossibly soft, pillows arranged with the kind of care that speaks of devotion. It's not furniture. It's an invitation.

Stellan steps deeper into the room, his voice low and musing. "It's not just responding to her. It's building itself around her." He pauses, gray eyes sweeping the space with something between awe and unease. "Whatever she wants—even if she doesn't know it yet."

The words land heavy in the charged air.

Bree stiffens beside me. Her eyes flick between the glowing walls, the abundance of pillows, the sheer size of the bed. "That's not—" she starts, but doesn't finish. Because we're all staring. And the bed is enormous.

Her shoulders curl inward like she wants to disappear into the floor.

"Holy shit," Jace breathes into the loaded silence. Then, louder: "Is this... is this a group bed situation? Because I'm going to need a seating chart."

Wes lets out a dry laugh. "Forget seating. We're gonna need a choreography guide."

"This is worse than the pancakes," Jace says to Bree, mock-serious but not unkind.

Bree's face flames red. "Can you all please stop talking?"

But Stellan isn't done. The smirk fades. Just a flicker. But it's the first crack in his mask I've ever seen. His voice carries something between appreciation and something darker. "Some houses are built for order. This one..." His gaze lingers on the bed, on the way the Ether pools around Bree's feet like it's claiming her. "Was clearly built for pleasure."

"Stellan," Bree warns, her voice small but sharp.

He raises his hands in mock surrender, but his expression has shifted completely now. Not teasing anymore. Something more serious. More unsettled. "She didn't build this with intention," he says quietly. "The Ether did it for her. Which means it knows her." His voice drops even lower. "And it believes she'll let herself be loved."

The silence that follows is deafening.

Bree stands by the bed, and I watch something flicker across her expression as she takes in its size, its implications. Not fear—something closer to wonder. Or disbelief. Like the room saw every piece of her heart—every hurt, every hope—and decided to make space for all of them. Even the ones shaped like us.

Her shoulders dip—just slightly. Like she's waiting to be told it's a mistake. Her fingers twist in the hem of her shirt, trying to hold herself small inside a moment that keeps asking her to take up space.

I cross the room without thinking, drawn by the need to ground her when she's spiraling. "They're just trying to catch up with what the Ether already knows," I say gently.

When I reach her side, she starts to speak.

"It's too much," she begins, voice small.

I stop her with a gentle touch at her wrist. "You don't have to earn this."

She looks up at me, green eyes wide with something between gratitude and disbelief. Like no one's ever told her she deserves good things just for existing.

I rest my hand on the edge of the bed, and the Ether responds immediately. It flows from around Bree's ankles toward my touch, pulses once—warm and welcoming and somehow approving. Silver script on the walls flares brighter for a moment, then settles into a gentle glow.

"You don't have to know what comes next," I tell her. "Just know that we're not afraid of it."

The others slowly find their places in the room. Rhett enters last, arms crossed, expression unreadable. But he doesn't leave. Just takes his position in the loose circle forming around the bed, around her.

Stellan doesn't sit with us, but he doesn't leave either. He leans against the far wall, unreadable, watching everything. Not judging. Just... observing. Like he's cataloging every gesture, every glance, every breath.

Around us.

Bree sits on the edge of the massive bed, and the fabric seems to welcome her, adjusting to her weight like it's been waiting centuries for this moment. We form a half-circle around her—not reverent, not afraid, just present.

I settle into a spot that feels like it was made for me, and realize with a start that it probably was. The visions never showed me this part—the quiet after the revelation, the simple rightness of being together in a space that finally feels like home.

But as I watch the Ether flow gently between us all, connecting and choosing and strengthening, I understand something the dreams never revealed.

This place wasn't built for power.

It was built for her.

And somehow... for us.

The circle holds. Not just the room. Not just the bed. But us.

Chapter 26
BREE

I stand in the doorway of the bedroom—my bedroom—looking back at the circular chamber we walked through to get here.

It's different now. The same curved walls rising to the domed ceiling, the same silver script pulsing like a gentle heartbeat. But something has changed while we were inside. Seven doors now stand around the perimeter, spaced along the curved walls where before there was only smooth stone. Each one glows faintly with something warmer than light. More personal.

I walk slowly across the polished floor, drawn by wonder and something deeper. Something that makes my chest feel full in a way I've never experienced.

The first door pulses with steady heat, warm stone framed with symbols that look like flames frozen mid-dance. Rhett's door. The sanctuary somehow knowing he needs a space that won't burn under his touch.

Next to it, another door practically vibrates with restless energy. Pale wood carved with flowing lines that suggest wind and movement. Jace's door, for someone who needs space to move and think and probably throw knives when the world gets too loud.

A door of polished dark wood catches my eye—no ornamentation, just smooth craftsmanship that speaks of quiet competence. Gray's door. For someone who finds peace in steady, reliable things.

The fourth door makes my breath catch. The frame is covered in symbols that seem to shift when I'm not looking directly—flowing script that might be prophecy or poetry. Theo's door, for someone who sees patterns in everything.

At the far end, a door that makes my chest tight with recognition. Warm wood carved with intricate designs that suggest growing things, but there's something else too—symbols that speak of emptiness waiting to be filled. Wes's door.

And then there are two more.

One made of silver-veined black stone, elegant and somehow predatory. The other carved from pale wood that seems to shimmer with its own inner light. I don't understand why they're here, but something in my stomach flutters when I look at them.

Something shifts in my chest when the mist touches that shimmering pale door. Not fear, exactly. More like... exposure. Like being seen in a way I'm not ready for. I try not to think about it.

"Well," Jace says behind me, "this is either really cool or really weird."

I turn to find him staring at his door with something between appreciation and concern. "So, uh, anyone want to guess why mine looks like it belongs in a high-security training facility?"

Wes appears beside him, looking at his own door with quiet intensity. "Hey, if this door is based on what I need, does that mean it has snacks and an industrial-strength lock?"

"Probably a whole kitchen," Rhett says, emerging from the bedroom. "And soundproofing."

The easy banter should make me laugh. Instead, heat crawls up my neck as I realize what this means. The Ether didn't just create space for me—it created space for all of them. Because it somehow knows what I want before I do.

"I didn't mean for..." I start, then stop. Because how do you explain that your magic apparently has opinions about everyone you care about?

"What if we add someone new?" Jace asks, grinning. "Does it just pop up another door?"

"The Ether will adjust," a voice says quietly from behind us. "That's what it does."

We all turn. Stellan stands at the entrance to the chamber, gray eyes taking in the doors with something unreadable in his expression. His gaze lingers on the pale shimmering door—the one that made my chest flutter—and something passes across his face too quickly to catch.

"It responds to connection," he continues, voice careful. "To... need."

The words hang heavy in the charged air, and I feel that flutter again when his eyes meet mine for just a moment before looking away.

Thane appears beside him, silver gaze cataloging the doors with typical precision. When he sees the black stone door, his jaw tightens almost imperceptibly.

"Seven," he says quietly.

"Should there be more?" Theo asks, stepping out from his own doorway. "Or fewer?"

"There should be exactly as many as there are," Stellan answers, but there's something in his tone that makes me think he's not entirely comfortable with his own inclusion.

Before anyone can respond, something shifts in my chest. Not painful—more like a gentle tug, like someone calling my name from very far away. I press my hand to my sternum, where the sensation seems to originate.

"Someone's here," I say, the words slipping out before I understand them.

Theo's expression sharpens. "What do you mean?"

"I don't know." I'm already moving, drawn by instinct I don't recognize. "But someone's at the door."

I pass the others as I walk, feeling their attention like weight on my shoulders.

Thane appears just behind me, his voice low but firm. "We've got her."

The guys hesitate—Rhett half a step forward, Wes tense in the doorway, Jace watching me like he might follow anyway.

But one by one, they nod. Not fully at ease. But trusting.

Behind me, I hear footsteps—Thane and Stellan falling into step, shadows drawn by something they can't name either.

The front entrance reveals itself as I approach—a door I'm certain wasn't visible before, made of pale wood banded with silver that gleams in the warm light. My hand rises, drawn without hesitation.

"Wait—" Thane's voice cuts through the air, sharp and low. Protective. Commanding.

But I don't. I don't *want* to wait.

I touch the handle.

Behind me, Stellan chuckles under his breath. "Of course she does."

And then I pull the door open.

A small family stands at the threshold, and my breath catches in my throat.

The woman is perhaps forty, with weathered hands and kind eyes that crinkle at the corners. Her partner stands beside her—broad-shouldered and solid, with the quiet strength of someone who works with his hands. And between them, a boy who can't be more than sixteen, all wide eyes and uncertain hope.

The boy sees it first—the Ether pulsing gently around me, yet still calm, almost expectant. He whispers something urgent to his parents, pointing.

And then, all three of them kneel.

"Please, please don't do that," I stammer, stepping back. "Get up, I don't—"

"You're the Source," the woman says, voice thick with emotion. "The one who called us home."

"I didn't call anyone," I protest, but my voice sounds small even to me. "I'm not—I still don't know what this place even is."

The woman rises slowly, tears streaming down her cheeks. "But you are. The Ether wouldn't have awakened if you weren't." She reaches out like she wants to touch me, then stops herself. "Most didn't believe it was real. Said the old bloodlines were gone, that the sanctuaries would never wake again. But we heard your call, love. Clear as anything."

She gestures to her family. "We'll earn our keep. I cook—I'm good at it, learned from my grandmother before her hands gave out. My husband can work the land, fix what needs fixing. The boy'll do whatever's needed."

The man nods—quiet, respectful. The boy stands taller, pride flickering through his nervousness.

"We didn't come to be served," she finishes. "We came to serve something that's been waiting a long, long time."

My chest tightens. *Not this. Not more people expecting me to lead something I don't understand. Not kindness I haven't earned.*

I take a half step back, voice cracking. "I don't—I don't have anywhere to put you. I don't even know how to—"

The words die in my throat as the Ether responds.

A ribbon of silver mist curls out from around my feet, flowing across the garden path like water following a channel. We all watch, breath held, as it slips between the trees and gathers over a patch of empty earth.

The mist swirls once, twice, then slowly dissipates.

In its place stands a small house.

It's modest but beautiful—stone walls that match the sanctuary, windows that catch the afternoon light, a door painted the same blue as the sky. Like it's always been there. Like it belongs.

The woman gasps, pressing both hands to her mouth. Her partner reaches out blindly, gripping her shoulder for support. The boy just stares, mouth hanging open.

The woman steps forward, eyes shining with tears.

"We meant it—we'll earn our keep," she says, voice trembling but sure.

I try to speak, but emotion clogs my throat. Because this—people wanting to stay, wanting to help, wanting to build something together—undoes something in me I didn't know was broken.

I nod, smiling shakily. "Okay. Then welcome home."

The woman starts crying in earnest then, and her partner's stern expression softens into something approaching disbelief. The boy grins like I've just handed him the sun.

"I'm Mairen," the woman says, wiping her eyes. "This is my husband Torn, and our son Kellan. We've been searching for so long..."

"How did you find us?" I ask.

"The Ether led us," Torn says simply. His voice is quiet, gruff with disuse. "Started a week ago. Felt like... like coming home."

"We packed everything we owned," Kellan adds, excitement making his voice crack. "Mom said we might be walking into nothing, but the pull was too strong to ignore."

I glance back and find Thane standing just inside the threshold, his expression carefully neutral. Watchful. Guarded.

And beside him, Stellan—still and silent, his gray eyes fixed not on the house, but on me.

"Stellan," I say softly, moving toward him. "They said they wanted to help. I couldn't say no."

He doesn't answer right away. His gaze flicks between me and the family, then to the house that appeared from mist and will alone. He watches Mairen's tears, the boy's awe. The miracle of it—unasked for, undeserved.

"No," he says finally, his voice lower than I've ever heard it. "Of course you couldn't."

There's no mockery in it. No edge. Just something quiet. Measured. Like he's observing something he never expected to witness.

The family begins moving toward the house, their footsteps soft on the garden path. Mairen talks gently to Kellan as he runs ahead, Torn following behind them, head bowed. Like they're giving us the moment. Or maybe the Ether is.

I want to say more—to explain, or maybe to ask—but the words don't come.

So I walk with them instead, silver mist rising gently around my feet in response to their joy. And as the sun dips toward the trees, I turn back toward the sanctuary.

The mist curls up through the light like breath.

And for once, I don't flinch.

For the first time in my life, I'm building something that lasts.

Chapter 27
BREE

I wake up alone in the circular bed, and for a moment, I forget where I am.

The room is soft with morning light filtering through the dome above. The walls still hold their gentle glow, silver script pulsing faintly like a sleeping heartbeat. The bed itself seems to exhale around me.

When I sit up, I notice things that weren't there last night.

A mug on the bedside shelf—my favorite mug, the chipped blue one from the apartment I don't want to remember. Soft slippers beside the bed that I definitely didn't pack. Rhett's sweatshirt draped over a chair, though I don't remember him leaving it there.

The Ether is still building for me. Still paying attention to what I need before I know I need it.

It should be unsettling. Instead, it feels like being held.

I pad across the room in the gifted slippers, pulling on Rhett's sweatshirt from where he left it draped over the chair. It's perfectly oversized, perfectly soft, and smells like him—cedar and warmth and something indefinably safe.

It hangs low on my thighs, brushing just past the tops. I know I'm wearing shorts underneath, but it doesn't exactly look like it. And I don't bother fixing that.

The old me would've covered up. I'm not sure I feel quite like old me anymore.

The sanctuary hallway opens before me as I walk, doorways revealing themselves with warm light. I don't question it anymore. This place knows me, and I'm starting to know it back.

I catch a glimpse of myself in the polished metal panel by the hall—bare legs, Rhett's sweatshirt, hair still sleep-tousled. I should go back and grab pants. I don't.

Let them look. I don't think my scars are meant to be hidden anymore.

The kitchen, when I find it, steals my breath.

Gray's already there—leaning against the counter, mug in hand.

His eyes lift at the sound of my footsteps... and then lower.

They linger, just for a second, on my bare legs.

Then flick up too fast, like he's ashamed to have looked at all. Like he caught himself breaking a rule.

Something flickers in my chest. Not anger exactly. Not shame. Just... something sharp.

He looked, and then he looked away. And somehow that hurts more than if he hadn't looked at all.

I don't know what I expected. Maybe nothing. Maybe just... not that.

"Morning," he says, suddenly fascinated by the inside of his coffee mug.

I don't answer. Not right away.

Something folds tight in my chest, and I don't know how to name it.

So I breathe in. Look around. Anchor myself to what's real.

Sunlight pours through tall windows wrapped in flowering vines. The counters are smooth gray stone, warm to the touch. An old hearth glows with gentle flame that doesn't seem to need fuel. A large island sits in the center—familiar in its proportions, like the sanctuary remembered how we used to gather around the kitchen table back home. Everything is beautiful in that way that feels both ancient and perfectly maintained.

And the pantry is full.

Baskets of fruit that look like they were picked this morning. Loaves of bread that smell like they just came from an oven I can't see. Fresh eggs in a bowl, milk in glass bottles, herbs hanging in bundles that fill the air with green scent.

I should question where it all came from. Should worry about magic I don't understand providing things I didn't ask for.

Instead, I just feel grateful.

I decide to make breakfast. Something simple—toast and eggs for whoever wakes up hungry. It's the least I can do after... everything. After they followed me here, after they saw the bed the Ether built and didn't run away.

But the toaster, when I find it, doesn't look like any toaster I've ever seen. It's made of the same warm stone as the counters, with symbols carved into its surface that glow faintly when I touch them.

I put bread in anyway. Press what looks like it might be the right symbol.

The bread disappears in a flash of silver light.

"Okay," I say to myself. "Not that one."

I try again with new bread, a different symbol. This time the bread comes back... black. Smoking. Definitely not edible.

The eggs don't go much better. The magical stove seems to have opinions about temperature that don't match mine. What should be a simple scramble turns into something that might generously be called abstract art.

I'm standing there with a smoking pan and the distinct smell of culinary failure when I realize Gray hasn't moved.

He's still leaning against the counter, mug in hand—but he's watching me now.

Eyes tracking the mess I've made like he's trying to decide whether to intervene or let me work it out myself.

Then his gaze drops again.

Not by accident this time.

It lingers—not long, not leering, just... held.

Like he's not fighting it as hard this time. Like some part of him is tired of pretending not to look.

When his eyes meet mine again, there's something unsteady in them. A quiet apology, maybe. Or regret for hiding it the first time.

I don't look away.

He meets my eyes and clears his throat. "Need a hand?

Before I can answer, he crosses to the toaster, reaching around me to press a different symbol.

His chest brushes lightly against my back—barely a touch, but enough to feel the heat of him.

It lights something sharp and unfamiliar under my skin.

He doesn't move right away. Just stands there, close and careful, like he's trying not to spook me.

Almost too careful.

The toaster chimes softly, and a perfect slice of golden toast pops up.

"I didn't mean to crowd you," he says quietly, voice low and close to my ear.

"You didn't." I swallow. "I just... I'm not used to this."

"To what?"

I turn in the small space between him and the counter, hand still on the pan, and suddenly we're closer than we've ever been.

Close enough to see the gold flecks in his green eyes.

Close enough to notice the scar along his jaw I've never asked about.

Close enough that my pulse forgets what it's supposed to do.

"To help," I admit. "To someone stepping in when things go wrong.

Something shifts in his expression. Something gentle and fierce all at once. "You don't have to do everything alone anymore."

He reaches past me again, this time for the pan of experimental eggs. His fingers brush mine on the handle, and I don't pull away. For a moment, we're both still—his hand covering mine, the morning light catching the gold in his eyes.

"I've got it," he says simply.

Then he takes the pan gently, scrapes the disaster into the waste bin, starts fresh.

I should move. Give him space to work. Instead, I lean against the counter and watch his hands—steady, sure, careful with everything he touches.

My mom used to make eggs like that," I say, nodding toward the pan where he's building something that actually looks like breakfast. "Fluffy. Perfect."

Gray doesn't answer right away. Just stirs the eggs, careful and precise.

Then, quietly—*almost like it isn't meant to be heard—*

"She taught me."

I blink. "My mom?"

He nods. Still not looking at me. "You were sick. Stayed home from school. She didn't want to leave you alone, so... she made breakfast. Said eggs were the only thing you'd eat when you felt like that."

The memory tugs at the edges of my mind—warmth and toast and something soft on a tray—but I thought she made them. I always thought it was her.

"Wait—those eggs were... you?"

He finally meets my eyes. There's something tired in his expression. Honest and unguarded.

"She made the first ones. Showed me how to get them right. Then said if you were going to trust someone else to make them... it might as well be me."

My throat tightens.

I thought she was trying to stay close. That she'd sat with me that morning because she loved me.

But maybe it was more than that.

Maybe she was sharing a piece of herself—passing it to him, so I could still have it, even after she was gone.

"I didn't know," I whisper.

Gray shrugs like it's nothing. But he adds a little extra cheese, just the way I like it. Like maybe it's not nothing at all.

The Ether stirs around my ankles, responding to something in his voice. Or maybe to the way he's looking at me—like he sees the magic she was talking about, even if I don't understand it yet.

Footsteps on the stairs announce the arrival of others. Jace appears first, golden hair sticking up at impossible angles, followed by Wes looking at me like he's hungry and slightly desperate.

Jace whistles low under his breath. "Damn, B. If you were going for casual murder, it's working."

Wes blinks hard. "Wait, is that Rhett's sweatshirt?"

"I thought it was mine," Rhett mutters as he appears behind them, but there's no heat in it—just a quiet possessiveness he doesn't bother hiding.

Wes swallows loudly. "I'm gonna... get coffee." He nearly fumbles the mug, and Jace claps him on the back with an obnoxious grin.

"You good, bro?"

"Totally," Wes says, voice cracking slightly. "Totally good."

Theo doesn't comment when he appears, but his gaze lingers for a beat too long, curious and unreadable.

"Please tell me someone made coffee," Wes says, beelining for the counter where a pot is already waiting. Of course it is.

"And please tell me no one made Bree cook," Jace adds, taking in the scene. "Because last time she tried to make breakfast for all of us, we ended up ordering pizza at eight in the morning."

"Hey," I protest, but there's no heat in it. "That was one time."

"One memorable time," Rhett says, appearing with Theo close behind. He surveys the kitchen, noting the golden toast, the perfect eggs Gray is plating, the general lack of smoke alarms going off. "Good call letting Gray handle it."

"Okay, *but* let's not forget the curry night," Wes adds, already pouring his coffee. "That was basically art."

"True," Jace says, nudging me with his elbow. "You *did* redeem yourself with that. I'm still dreaming about it."

I duck my head, smiling despite myself. "That was different. I actually knew what I was doing."

"We noticed," Rhett says, voice softer now. "Still think about it sometimes.

Theo doesn't say anything, but he catches my eye and smiles—soft and
knowing and somehow proud.

They settle around the kitchen with the easy familiarity of people who've
done this before. Jace claims a stool at the counter. Wes hovers near the
coffee pot like it might disappear if he looks away. Rhett starts pulling
plates from cabinets that definitely weren't open yesterday but seem to be
expecting him now.

It's domestic and comfortable and everything I never thought I could
have, even in this new space.

That's when Thane walks in.

His gaze sweeps the room once—cataloging the group, the breakfast, the
comfort. Then it lands on me. He doesn't flinch, doesn't look away. Just
watches in that unblinking, measuring way of his. Like he's logging every
exposed inch of skin, not for desire—but for what it might cost.

He doesn't speak right away. But his jaw ticks.

"Morning," he says carefully, silver eyes still taking in the scene.

"Coffee's fresh," Gray offers, not looking up from the eggs he's dividing
between plates.

Thane nods but doesn't move toward the pot. Instead, he lingers near
the doorway, watching us with that assessing gaze that makes me feel like
he's cataloging everything for some report I'll never see.

Stellan appears behind him, and the temperature in the room seems to
shift.

Not dramatically. Not dangerously. Just... different.

He leans in the doorway, gray eyes sweeping the kitchen with something I can't identify. When his gaze lands on me, it's not sharp or hungry—it's unreadable. And I hate how much that unsettles me.

"Good morning," he says, voice carrying that familiar edge of amusement.

But the amusement doesn't reach his eyes. And when I offer him coffee, he doesn't quite meet my gaze.

"Morning," I manage, tugging the sweatshirt down a little like it'll help. It doesn't.

"It's more than I expected," he says quietly, still watching me.

"What is?"

He gestures vaguely at the kitchen, at the perfectly brewed coffee and magically stocked pantry and the way everyone moves around each other like pieces of a puzzle finding their places.

"This," he says. "All of it."

There's something in his tone that makes my stomach clench. Not quite approval, not quite concern. Something heavier.

Breakfast proceeds with careful conversation—Jace making observations about magical appliances, Wes inhaling food like he hasn't eaten in days, Theo quietly helping clear plates while catching my eye with small, encouraging smiles. Rhett positions himself where he can see all the exits, still protective even here. Normal things that feel surreal in this ancient place that's rearranging itself around my subconscious.

Stellan barely eats. Doesn't talk much, either, though I can feel something strange in the room—like the energy is humming just beneath the surface. Jace's laughter, Wes's restlessness, the warmth between everyone else... it *should* feel like enough. But Stellan just watches, like none of it touches him

He brushes past me to refill his coffee, and the distance feels deliberate. Like the kitchen is too warm for him.

Instead, he watches. Catalogues. Pulls away.

When the last plate is cleared and conversations start to wind down, he stands.

Thane's still near the wall, arms crossed. Watching. Still.

The room goes quiet.

"I'll be leaving this morning," Stellan says, smooth and matter-of-fact.

My coffee mug stops halfway to my lips. "What?"

He sets the cup down with quiet precision. "There are things I need to tend to. Council threads to pull before they tighten."

There's no tension in his voice, but something about the phrasing lands wrong.

"Now?" I ask.

"It's better if I'm not here for what comes next." His smile is faint and polished. "You've made this place yours. The rest of it doesn't need me."

"Stellan." I rise without thinking. "You don't have to—"

"I know." He cuts me off gently. "But I'm going anyway."

I step forward, unsure what I'm reaching for. "If it's about something I did—"

"You didn't." His voice softens. Almost warm. "That's not why I'm leaving."

He doesn't offer more than that. Just gives a slight bow of his head—formal, final.

Then he turns toward the others and nods once. Respectful. Measured. He meets Thane's gaze last.

"Be well, Brielle."

And then he walks out.

The silence he leaves behind settles like fog.

I stare at the doorway, trying to make sense of the hollowness in my chest.

Behind me, I hear Thane shift. When I glance back, he's already looking at me.

Not suspicious. Not cold.

Just... watching.

Then he turns without a word and follows Stellan out.

Chapter 28
THANE

The door closes behind Stellan with a soft click that echoes louder than it should in the morning quiet.

I watch Bree for a long moment through the kitchen window. She's still sitting at the table in Rhett's sweatshirt, hands wrapped around her coffee mug like it's anchoring her to something solid. Her hair is still messy from sleep, and when Wes says something that makes her laugh, the sound carries through the glass like a bell.

She looks... settled. Happy, even.

The sight of it twists something in my chest that I don't want to name.

I turn without a word and follow Stellan out.

The morning air is crisp, charged with the kind of magic that clings to sacred places. The sanctuary's grounds stretch ahead of us—pale stone paths winding between ancient trees that shouldn't be flowering this late in the season but are anyway. Everything here responds to her, reshapes itself around her presence like the world is trying to make itself worthy.

Stellan is already halfway down the main path when I catch sight of him, moving with that liquid grace he's perfected over centuries.

I don't call out. Just track him through the dappled shadows, my footsteps silent on stone that hums faintly beneath my boots.

When I finally speak, my voice cuts through the morning stillness like a blade.

"You don't run. That's never been your style."

He doesn't stop walking. Doesn't even slow down.

"It's not running if there's nothing chasing you."

The casual dismissal hits exactly where he meant it to. "No. You just couldn't stand that it didn't revolve around you."

That makes him pause. Just for a breath. But he keeps walking.

Trees close around us as the path descends, their branches forming a canopy that filters the light into shifting patterns. The kind of beauty that should be peaceful. Instead, it feels like walking into a trap.

"You left because it felt too real," I say, letting my voice carry the accusation he's trying to avoid. "Because she didn't need you to hold the center."

Stellan stops walking.

The silence stretches between us, heavy with centuries of understanding that's never been spoken aloud. When he finally turns, there's something raw in his expression that I've only seen once before—the night he found me half-dead in an alley, fangs still bloody from feeding on someone who hadn't consented.

"No," he says quietly. "I left because I saw myself in you. And that scared me more."

The words land wrong, cutting deeper than they should. "What the hell does that mean?"

His gray eyes are steady, unflinching. "You're still waiting for the version of her that fixes you. And when you realized she was real—kind, wounded, human—you couldn't look at her."

I want to deny it. Want to throw back some cutting response that will put distance between us and this conversation. But the words stick.

"She's not what I expected," I say finally.

"No?" Stellan's tone is careful now. Probing.

"No." The admission costs me. "I expected a weapon. Got offered breakfast instead."

The memory surfaces before I can stop it—that morning, the way she held my gaze when I mentioned the journey ahead. Not afraid. Not grateful. Just measuring. Like she was deciding if I was worth the effort.

"She looked at me like..." I stop. Cut the thought off before it goes somewhere I can't take back.

Stellan waits.

"Like I might be useful," I finish. Safe. Clinical. Not the truth.

Stellan's mask slips for just a moment, pain flickering across his features before he locks it down again. But not fast enough.

"Someone like you," he repeats, and there's something sharp in his tone now. "You still think every bond can be earned through suffering. Or worse—taken. You're a vampire, Thane. You take. That's what they'll always see when they look at you."

The word hangs in the air between us like a curse. *Vampire.* The first time either of us has said it aloud in decades.

I flinch—just barely, but enough for him to see.

"And you?" I fire back, letting my own venom surface. "You don't even feed. You seduce and call it mercy."

"At least I don't—"

A quiet sound interrupts him. A branch snapping. The soft intake of breath.

We both turn.

Theo stands a few yards back on the path, those deep brown eyes wide with something that looks like recognition. His chest rises and falls too quickly, like he's been running, but he's perfectly still.

For a moment, nobody moves. Nobody speaks.

Then Theo's voice cuts through the tension, quiet but carrying unexpected steel.

"You're both idiots."

I try to regain my footing, fall back on the authority that's kept me alive for centuries. "This isn't your—"

"Shut up."

The words are quiet, but they carry weight. Command. Like he's finally found his voice and decided to use it.

Theo steps forward, and I can see something shifting in his expression—the careful, thoughtful mind that's been watching and cataloging everything finally reaching a conclusion.

"You talk about her like she's a prophecy," he says, voice gaining strength with each word. "Like she's something to claim or be afraid of. She's not."

Another step forward. The morning light catches something fierce in his brown eyes.

"She's Bree. She's the one who asked me to help when everything was falling apart. Who trusted me enough to let me see her scared. Who thanked me after." His voice wavers slightly, but doesn't break. "She makes space for all of us, even when no one made space for her. And you... both of you... got scared the moment you felt it pulling back."

The pain in his voice is raw, immediate. Like he's speaking from wounds that are still healing.

"You keep arguing about whether you deserve her—like that's yours to decide. But it's not. She already chose. Even if she doesn't realize it yet."

He looks directly at me, and there's something in his expression that makes me want to step backward. Not fear. Certainty.

"You want to know what real is? She is. That's what scared you. Both of you."

The accusation settles over me like ice water. Because he's right, and we all know it.

Theo pauses, glances between us, and when he speaks again, his voice is softer. More careful.

"And maybe it's not my story to tell. But there are things you need to know. About where she came from. About what she survived."

Something shifts in his posture, in the set of his shoulders. Like he's gathering courage for something difficult.

"About why the Ether didn't just find her—it chose her."

The words hang in the morning air, weighted with implications I'm not ready to face. Beside me, Stellan has gone perfectly still, that predatory alertness that means he's cataloging threats.

But Theo isn't done.

"She doesn't need saving," he says, and there's steel in his voice now. Certainty that cuts through every excuse I've been making. "But she deserves people who won't run the second they feel something. Who won't flinch when she lets them see the truth."

He turns then, starts walking back toward the sanctuary. Back toward her.

After a few steps, he stops. Doesn't turn around.

"What do you know about what she is?" I ask, my voice rougher than I intended.

Theo glances back over his shoulder, and for a moment, he looks older than his years. Tired in a way that has nothing to do with sleep.

"Enough to know she carries more than anyone should. And still chooses softness. If that scares you, you were never the one she needed."

Then he's gone, disappearing around the bend in the path like he was never there at all.

I watch the space where he vanished, trying to process what just happened. Trying to understand how the quiet one among them just stripped me bare with a handful of words.

Stellan and I stand in the growing silence, neither of us willing to be the first to speak.

Finally, he breaks.

"He's not wrong."

"No," I admit, the word scraping against my throat. "He's not."

"So what now?"

I don't answer immediately. Can't answer immediately. Because for the first time in centuries, I'm not sure I know.

What I do know is this: I came here to assess a threat. To determine if Bree Holloway was the weapon the Council feared she might be. To decide if she needed to be controlled or eliminated.

Instead, I found a girl who tries to make breakfast and doesn't flinch when she looks at me.

That's a problem I wasn't prepared for.

"I don't know," I say finally.

Stellan nods, like he expected that answer. Like he's been asking himself the same question.

We stand there in the dappled morning light, two predators who've spent centuries learning how to survive in a world that sees us as expendable. As dangerous. As less than.

And for the first time, I wonder if maybe the problem isn't that we're not worthy of her.

Maybe the problem is that we've never learned how to be worthy of ourselves.

The thought follows me as I start walking back toward the sanctuary. Back toward the girl who offered me coffee like it was nothing.

Back toward the moment when I'll have to decide what kind of operative I want to be when she looks at me again.

It's not Bree I have to earn, I realize.

It's the right to stay.

After a few steps, I glance back at Stellan. He's still standing in the dappled light, perfectly still.

"You coming?"

Chapter 29
BREE

The door swings open so fast it nearly slams against the wall.

"I'm so sorry, darling—I missed breakfast, didn't I?" Mairen bustles in with an apron half-tied and cheeks flushed, scanning the kitchen like she expects to find me still stirring eggs. "I've got a new batch going, don't you worry—"

I blink, halfway to rinsing my mug. "We already ate."

She stops short, blinking owlishly. "You did?" A beat. Then, cheerfully: "Oh, well. Plenty of mouths still to feed."

My frown deepens. "What do you mean?"

She smiles, wiping her hands on her apron like it's the most ordinary thing in the world. "The ones that came, dear."

She gestures vaguely toward the front of the house.

"They're all outside. Because of you."

My breath catches. "Outside?"

The woman nods, entirely unfazed. "Mm-hmm. I'd say about a hundred or so, maybe more. Quiet as anything, just standing there. Like they've been waiting."

"Waiting for what?" Rhett asks, straightening from where he's been wiping down the counter.

The woman's eyes twinkle. "You, darling. Or rather, her."

Jace lets out a low whistle. "Well, that's not ominous at all."

Theo's already moving toward the front windows. "She said they're outside?"

"I didn't hear any cars," Wes mutters, looking suddenly uneasy.

"They didn't drive," Mairen says simply. "They *followed the Ether*."

That draws a silence thicker than surprise—something heavier, older, crawling under my skin like static.

I glance around. The others are already in motion.

"Come on," Gray says, his voice quieter than usual. "Let's see what we're dealing with."

No one asks if we should.

We just go.

The hallway stretches ahead of us as we move toward the front of the sanctuary. Theo appears from somewhere behind us, slightly out of breath.

"Where were you?" Jace asks, falling into step beside him.

"Went out the back," Theo says, pushing his hair out of his eyes. "Thought I heard something. Didn't see anything, though."

"Following Stellan and Thane?" Jace's tone carries just enough knowing edge to make Theo flush slightly.

"Just... checking," Theo mutters.

I catch Wes's expression as we walk—something restless in the set of his shoulders, the way his eyes keep darting between the front door and back toward where Theo came from. Like he's caught between wanting to know what happened and being afraid of the answer.

There's something different about him lately. More... awake, somehow. Like he's been sleepwalking for years and is finally starting to stir. I want to ask him about it, but the front door is already in sight.

The front door opens to something that steals my breath completely.

The sanctuary grounds stretch out in gentle slopes of pale stone and flowering trees, beautiful in the morning light. But the beauty isn't what stops me cold.

It's the people.

Mairen wasn't kidding.

They cover the lawn like a sea of stillness—maybe a hundred, maybe more. Men and women of every age, standing in loose clusters or sitting on the grass. Some look like they've been traveling for days. Others seem like they just stepped out of normal lives and found themselves here.

But they're all looking at me.

The moment we step fully into view, the entire crowd drops to their knees.

Not quickly. Not dramatically. Just... naturally. Like breathing. Like they've been waiting for this exact moment their entire lives.

The silence is so complete I can hear my own heartbeat.

"Holy shit," Jace breathes beside me.

I can't move. Can't speak. The weight of a hundred pairs of eyes, all focused on me with something that looks like reverence, presses down until I can barely breathe.

"I didn't ask for this," I whisper.

The mist starts to curl around my ankles—not thick or dramatic, just a whisper of silver that moves as if it's trying to comfort me in response to my panic. But even that small movement draws murmurs from the crowd. Awe. Recognition.

Rhett positions himself slightly in front of me, protective instincts kicking in. Gray hangs back but I can feel his attention like a weight. Wes looks pale, his jaw tight with something that might be fear.

Theo, though. Theo is smiling. Just slightly. Like he's been expecting this.

"You knew," I say, not really a question.

"I had... an idea," he admits. "The visions have been getting stronger. More specific. People on roads, all moving toward the same place."

"And you didn't think to mention it?"

"Would it have changed anything?" His voice is gentle. "Would you have been more ready if you'd known?"

I look out at the sea of kneeling figures and know he's right. Nothing could have prepared me for this.

That's when one figure stands.

The first thing I notice is how she moves—confident without being threatening, like she's used to being looked at but doesn't need the attention. Dark skin, hair that shines in the morning light. There's something familiar about her, though I know we've never met.

She walks forward alone, and I tense slightly—but then she makes herself smaller somehow. Not like she's afraid, just... careful. Like she knows everyone's watching and doesn't want to spook me.

When she's close enough to speak quietly, she says, "Looks like someone forgot your throne, sweetheart."

I blink, startled. "Do I know you?"

She smiles, and some of the tension in my shoulders eases. "Not yet. But I have a feeling we're going to be good friends. I'm Zira, by the way."

"I'm Bree," I manage, though something tells me she already knows that.

Behind me, I hear Theo make a small sound of agreement. When I glance back, he's nodding slightly, that knowing look in his eyes.

I don't know why, but that doesn't worry me the way it probably should. There's something about her—the way she's looking at me like I'm a person instead of whatever these other people think I am.

I feel that pull again—the same one I get around Thane and Stellan and... Wes. But where the others make me feel uncertain or overwhelmed, this feels... steadying. Like recognition without the weight.

"We've come from all over," she continues, gesturing back toward the crowd without taking her eyes off me. "Different paths, same call. The Ether, it... pulled. And we followed."

"I don't understand," I say, my voice barely above a whisper.

"You don't have to understand it yet. You just have to feel where it's leading." Her smile softens. "They want to hear from you, you know."

The thought sends ice through my veins. "I don't have anything to say."

She tilts her head, and for a second, I think she might laugh. But her expression stays gentle. "Say that, then. Say anything. You don't have to command the room. Just let them know you see them."

I look back at the others. Rhett nods once, firm and steady. Jace gives me an encouraging smile even though I can see the worry in his eyes. Gray's expression is unreadable, but he's not moving away. Theo's still smiling that knowing smile.

Wes looks scared, but when our eyes meet, he nods too.

"You got this," Jace whispers.

Do I?

I don't feel like I've got anything. I feel like a girl who was eating breakfast twenty minutes ago and now has a hundred strangers staring at her like she's supposed to save them from something.

But they're all looking at me. Waiting.

And maybe... maybe that's enough.

I take a step forward.

The crowd shifts slightly, attention sharpening, but no one stands. No one speaks.

Another step. The mist follows, curling gently around my feet like it's trying to give me courage.

By the time I reach the edge of the stone terrace that overlooks the lawn, my heart is pounding so hard I'm sure everyone can hear it.

Behind me, Zira's voice is quiet but clear. "That's it, babe. Just let them see your eyes."

I open my mouth to speak.

Chapter 30
BREE

I take a breath and step forward to the edge of the stone terrace.

The silence is complete. A hundred faces turned up toward me, waiting. Behind me, I can feel the guys' tension like a physical weight, but I'm doing this. Finding my way through on my own.

My voice comes out smaller than I meant it to, but it carries in the stillness.

"I don't know what's happening."

The honesty hangs in the air between us. I see a few people exchange glances, but no one moves. No one speaks.

"I didn't ask for this," I continue, my voice growing steadier. "But... I'm trying to understand it."

The Ether curls gently around my ankles, responding to something quiet and sure inside me. Not dramatic. Just... present.

"You're welcome here," I say, looking out over the sea of faces. "We'll try to make space for everyone."

I pause, searching for words that feel true.

"I'm not a leader. I'm not royalty. But if you're here because of the Ether..." I swallow hard. "Then I won't turn you away."

The Ether flickers like wind over a field, and for a moment, something shifts in the crowd. Not worship. Something quieter. Something that feels like hope.

Behind me, I sense Zira stepping closer. Grounding me in a way I didn't realize I needed.

That's when a voice cuts through the stillness.

"You speak like you're one of us—but you don't know what we've been through."

A man near the middle of the crowd pushes to his feet. He's thin, ragged around the edges, with the kind of hunger in his eyes that feels dangerous. The people around him shift away slightly, creating space.

I feel my chest tighten, but I force myself to stay steady. "You're right. I don't. But—"

"But nothing." He takes a step forward, and the air around him seems to crackle with aggressive energy. "You stand there in your pretty sanctuary, offering us scraps, and you think that makes you worthy?"

My mouth opens to respond, but the words never come.

Because he lunges.

The world slows and sharpens all at once. I see his face twist with hunger and rage, see the way his fingers curl like claws. He's fast—faster than human, faster than anything I've ever seen—and I'm frozen, my feet rooted to the stone.

Someone behind me shouts my name. The crowd gasps, some scrambling backward, others leaning forward. But I can't move, can't breathe, can't do anything but watch him close the distance between us.

He's three feet away when a flash of dark movement intercepts him mid-air.

Thane appears like he materialized from shadow, slamming into the attacker with brutal efficiency. The sound of the impact makes me flinch—bone meeting bone, the sharp exhale of air forced from lungs.

There's no hesitation in Thane's movements, no mercy. Just controlled violence, deadly and practiced. His fangs find the attacker's throat, and I hear the wet sound of punctured flesh, the man's sharp cry of pain and shock.

But the attacker doesn't go down easy. Even with Thane's fangs in his neck, he fights back, claws raking across Thane's ribs and tearing through fabric and flesh. The sound Thane makes—half growl, half grunt of pain—cuts through me like a blade.

Thane throws him aside with enough force that the man hits the ground hard and stays there. Unconscious. Bleeding from the throat but breathing.

The entire exchange takes maybe ten seconds. But it feels like a lifetime.

Gasps ripple through the crowd, but I don't hear them.

All I can see is Thane, still on the ground where they fought, one hand pressed to his side where dark stains are already spreading across his shirt.

I'm running before I realize I've moved.

"Thane—"

I drop to my knees beside him, hands reaching for him without thought. He tries to brush me off, his silver eyes sharp despite the pain.

"It's fine," he says through gritted teeth. "Just a scratch."

"Like hell it is." My hands find the tear in his shirt, and I press my palm against his side. The blood is warm, too warm, and I can feel how his breathing hitches when I touch him.

The Ether responds without my asking—not healing, just steadying. Like it's trying to hold him together until we can get him proper help.

Thane goes very still under my touch. His silver eyes find mine, and there's something vulnerable in them that I've never seen before.

"Bree," he says quietly. "You don't have to—"

"Yes, I do."

The words come out fierce, certain. And I realize they're true.

I pull my hand back, blood dark on my palm.

"Help me get him inside," I say, not sure who I'm talking to.

But they're already there—Rhett and Gray moving to support Thane's weight, Jace hovering nearby, Theo and Wes flanking us protectively. Zira moves to my side, helping me up from where I'm still kneeling, a look on her face that I'm not sure what it means.

She smirks. "Babe, you just changed everything."

Chapter 31
GRAY

The attack replays behind my eyelids every time I blink.

I'm standing in the doorway of Thane's room, arms crossed, trying to look casual while my mind runs though everything I should have done differently. Should have been faster. Should have seen it coming. Should have been the one between her and danger.

Instead, I froze.

And Thane moved.

The memory tastes bitter. The way he materialized from shadow, with his controlled violence and deadly precision. The wet sound of fangs finding flesh. The dark stains spreading across his shirt as he threw that Feeder aside like he weighed nothing.

I should be grateful. I am grateful.

But it burns anyway.

"You fanged out in front of a hundred Feeders," Stellan says from his spot against the dresser, voice dry as dust. He's watching Thane with something that might be amusement if it wasn't so calculating. "Subtle."

Thane shifts against the pillows, wincing slightly as the movement pulls at his bandages. Bree immediately leans closer, one hand hovering near his shoulder like she can't decide whether to touch or give him space.

"It was necessary," Thane says, but his tone lacks its usual edge. Soft. Almost gentle.

The change in him is unsettling. This isn't the controlled, strategic Thane who showed up at our door a little over a week ago. This version lets Bree fuss over him. Accepts her worry. Lets her see him bleed.

"Necessary," Stellan repeats, that knowing smirk tugging at his mouth. "Right. Had nothing to do with protective instincts."

"Stellan." The warning in Thane's voice should be terrifying. Now it just sounds tired.

"You just gave yourself away," Stellan continues, ignoring the warning entirely. "This isn't the Thane I know."

And that's the problem, isn't it? None of us are who we were.

Jace paces near the window, flipping knives in a steady rhythm that betrays his restless energy. Rhett stands silent in the corner, fists clenched, jaw tight with the kind of self-blame I recognize because it's eating me alive too.

Theo sits in the chair near the bed, calm but reading the room with that deeper insight of his. His eyes keep flicking between Bree and Thane, noticing something, though I have no idea what.

And Wes—

Wes leans against the doorframe beside me, arms crossed, tension radiating from every line of his body. But it's not the same tension the rest of us carry. His feels... hungrier. More aware.

Our eyes meet briefly, and something flickers between us. Heat. Recognition. The memory of the woods, of his mouth on mine, of the confusion that followed.

It hasn't come up again. We haven't talked about it.

But it's there. Waiting.

I look away first, focus on Bree instead. She's adjusting Thane's pillows with careful hands, and he's letting her. Actually letting her. The same man who as far as I can tell barely tolerates being touched is accepting her attention like it's oxygen.

That's when I notice it—the way Wes tracks her movements. It's not casual observation. Something deeper. His gaze follows the curve of her neck as she leans forward, the way her hair falls across her shoulder. When she laughs at something Stellan says, Wes's body goes still like he's listening to music.

But then his eyes flick to me, and there's something like fear in them. Like he knows I'm watching. Like he knows something's changing and he can't stop it.

The hunger. It's getting stronger.

I file the observation away, another piece of a puzzle I don't have all the pieces to yet. But I can feel the shape of it forming. The way magic pulls at all of us now. The way Bree's presence amplifies everything we thought we understood about ourselves.

The way none of us fit in our own skin anymore.

"I need some air," I say suddenly, pushing off from the doorframe.

"Gray—" Rhett starts, but I'm already moving.

I make it three steps down the hallway before Wes follows.

"Hey." His voice is quiet, careful. "You okay?"

I stop, hands flexing at my sides. Turn to face him.

He looks different in the soft light filtering through the sanctuary windows. Sharper somehow. More present. Like he's been sleepwalking for years and is finally starting to wake up.

There's something else too—something I can't quite put my finger on. His features seem more defined than they were weeks ago. The line of his jaw a little cleaner. His cheekbones a touch more pronounced. Still Wes, but like someone took an eraser to the softer edges and left behind something that catches the eye.

"Are you?" I ask instead of answering.

Something flickers across his expression. Uncertainty. Want. Fear.

"I don't know," he admits, voice barely above a whisper. "I feel... different. Like something's crawling under my skin. Like I'm hungry for something but I don't know how to feed it."

The honesty hits me harder than I expect. Because I understand. Maybe not the hunger, but the feeling of being unmade. Of watching pieces of yourself you thought were fixed start to shift and change.

"It's the magic," I say. "It's changing all of us."

"Is it?" His eyes search mine. "Or is it just showing us what was already there?"

The question hangs between us, heavy with implications I'm not ready to examine. Because if he's right—if this is who we've always been, just buried under years of denial and fear—then everything I thought I knew about myself is wrong.

"The woods, the stairs" I say suddenly.

Wes goes very still. "Gray—"

"I don't regret it."

The words come out before I can stop them, raw and honest in a way that makes my chest tight. Wes's eyes widen slightly, and I see the exact moment something in him shifts. Not breaking. Opening.

"I don't either," he breathes.

We stand there in the hallway, three feet apart, the air between us charged with possibility. With want and confusion and the growing certainty that whatever's happening to us isn't going to stop.

The sound of laughter from Thane's room breaks the moment. Bree's voice, warm and bright, followed by Jace's snort of amusement. Life continuing around us while we stand frozen in the space between what was and what might be.

"We should get back," Wes says, but he doesn't move.

"Yeah," I agree, but I don't move either.

Instead, I take a step closer. Close enough to see the way his pupils dilate slightly, the way his breathing changes. Close enough to catch that scent that's been driving me quietly insane for days—sandalwood and something deeper, something that makes my mouth water.

"Gray." My name sounds different in his voice. Like a prayer. Like a question.

Before I can respond—before I can do something stupid like kiss him again—footsteps echo from the main hallway. Multiple sets, moving with purpose.

"Sounds like Zira's back," Wes says, stepping back. The moment breaks, but the tension doesn't fade. If anything, it thickens.

"With food, probably," I add, grateful for the distraction and disappointed by it in equal measure.

We head back toward Thane's room, the space between us charged with unfinished conversation. But as we reach the doorway, I catch sight of something that stops me cold.

Bree is sitting on the edge of Thane's bed, one hand resting lightly on his forearm. It's a simple touch. Casual. The kind of contact she usually braces for.

But her hand doesn't shake. She doesn't flinch or pull away when he moves beneath her touch.

She trusts him. Completely. Unconsciously.

The realization hits me hard. Not because I'm jealous—though there's an edge of that too—but because it means something fundamental has shifted.

Bree isn't just surviving anymore.

She's choosing. Even if she doesn't realize it yet.

And as I watch, the mist curls lazily around her ankles, content and settled in a way I've never seen before.

Like it knows something the rest of us haven't figured out yet.

Zira's voice echoes from down the hall, bright and irreverent as she calls out something about feeding the wounded. Behind her, I can hear Kellan's quieter response, probably carrying whatever his mother insisted on sending.

The crisis is over. The room is settling back into something normal.

But everything has changed.

I catch Theo watching me from across the room, that small, knowing smile playing at his lips. Like he can see exactly what I'm thinking. What I'm realizing.

The attack was just the beginning.

Something's changing between all of us. Not just the magic. The way we move. The way we look at each other. Like gravity's been rewritten.

And for the first time since this all started, I'm not afraid of it.

I'm hungry for it.

"Better grab a plate," Zira announces as she sweeps into the room, arms full of containers that smell like heaven.

"Mom made enough to feed an army." Kellan appears behind her, grinning sheepishly as he sets down a tray of drinks. "She said warriors need proper nutrition."

The mood in the room shifts, lightens. Jace immediately gravitates toward the food. Rhett's shoulders loosen slightly. Even Thane accepts a water bottle without protest.

But I keep watching Bree. The way she laughs at something Zira says. The way her posture has relaxed completely. The way the mist around her feet seems to pulse in rhythm with her heartbeat.

She didn't flinch when I touched her.

That's all the proof I need.

The Ether knows. Even if she doesn't.

And whatever comes next—whatever we're all becoming—I'm ready for it.

All of it.

Even the parts that scare me.

Chapter 32
THEO

It's time.

Chapter 33
THEO

2:50 a.m.

Gray wakes first, like I knew he would. His eyes snap open the moment I touch his shoulder, sharp and immediately alert. No confusion, no disorientation. Just focus.

"Time?" he asks, voice barely a whisper.

"Soon," I murmur back. "Get dressed."

He nods and rolls out of bed in one fluid motion, already reaching for clothes. No questions. He trusts the visions, even when I can't explain them.

Wes is bleary when I shake him awake, blinking up at me with confusion that slowly sharpens into something like concern. His dark eyes search my face, looking for answers I don't have words for yet.

"Theo?" His voice is rough with sleep. "What's happening?"

"I need you to come with me," I say quietly. "Trust me?"

He sits up, runs a hand through his curls, but he's already moving. "Always."

The simple certainty in his voice does something strange to my chest. Warm and tight all at once.

Jace mutters something under his breath that sounds like profanity when I wake him, but his tone shifts the moment he sees my expression.

The joke dies on his lips, replaced by the kind of sharp attention that means he's reading the room.

"This isn't a drill, is it?" he asks, pulling on a t-shirt.

"No."

He nods once, grabs his knives from the nightstand. "Lead the way."

Rhett is already awake when I reach his door, sitting on the edge of his bed like he's been waiting. His hazel eyes find mine in the darkness, and I see the recognition there. The understanding that something's shifted.

"How long?" he asks.

"Not long enough."

He stands, shoulders already tense with the kind of controlled energy that makes the air around him feel warmer. "Then let's go."

I pause outside Bree's door, pulling a small piece of polished quartz from my pocket. It's nothing special—just a stone I've carried for years, now worn impossibly smooth by recent visions. But tonight it hums with protective intent as I set it carefully on the floor by her threshold.

A small ward. A whisper of safety while we handle what's coming.

The others watch silently as I straighten, understanding without explanation that some things require ritual. Some protections can't wait.

Thane's room glows softly when we approach, and I'm not surprised to find both him and Stellan already awake. Thane sits in the chair by the window, shirt half-unbuttoned over his healing bandages, silver eyes reflecting the dim light. Stellan lounges with his usual poised stillness, one leg crossed, watching Thane with lazy amusement.

They look up as we file in, and I see the exact moment Thane reads my expression. His entire posture shifts, sharpens.

"Forty-six minutes," I say without preamble.

Everyone goes still.

"Before they arrive."

"Who the hell is 'they'?" Jace asks, voice tight.

I meet his eyes, then look around the room at each of them in turn. Gray, alert and ready. Wes, confusion giving way to something darker. Rhett, coiled tension barely contained. Stellan, deceptively relaxed but listening to every word.

And Thane, watching me with an intensity that makes my skin warm.

"That's what we have to find out," I say. "Some aren't Feeders. Some are. Some might not come to join her—they might come to use her."

The words taste bitter, but they're true. I've seen fragments of it in dreams, felt the shape of threat approaching like storm clouds on the horizon.

But there's something else I've seen too. Something that cuts through the darkness of those visions like light.

"She's ready," I continue, and the certainty of it rings in my voice.

Thane straightens slightly. "For what?"

A beat of silence stretches between us.

I pause, letting the weight of what I'm about to say settle in my chest first. Because once I voice it, there's no taking it back. No pretending we don't all feel the pull, the magnetic certainty that's been building between us all.

"She's already chosen most of us," I say quietly. "Even if she doesn't realize it yet."

The reactions are immediate and telling.

Wes visibly shudders, like the words hit something raw and exposed. His hands flex at his sides, and I catch the way his breathing changes. Recognition mixed with fear.

Gray shows no surprise, just the quiet confirmation of something he's been seeing for himself. His jaw ticks once, but his eyes stay steady.

Jace grins like Christmas came early, all sharp edges and delighted anticipation. "Fucking finally," he breathes.

But it's Rhett who surprises me. His entire body goes rigid, hands clenching into fists as something dark and possessive flickers across his expression. Like hearing it said out loud ignited something he's been fighting to keep buried.

Thane goes very still, silver eyes fixed on me with an intensity that makes the air feel charged. Something shifts in his expression—not surprise, but recognition. Like he's been waiting for someone else to see what he's already known.

Stellan's mouth curves in that knowing way of his. "And what, exactly, does that have to do with me?"

The question hangs in the air, but I can see the answer in the way he's watching us all. He knows. They all know, on some level.

"She'll need us," I continue, voice softer now but no less certain. "All of us. In every way possible." I let that settle for a moment before adding, "Because whatever's coming—whoever's coming—they won't just be after her power."

That part hadn't been in the earlier visions, not clearly—but I felt it as soon as we stepped into the hallway tonight. Something was *moving*. A current already loosed from our control. Some of the people who witnessed the attack yesterday were already texting, calling, posting. And someone, somewhere, was listening.

It's already begun.

I give them a minute to let that sink in as I watch the understanding dawn in different ways across different faces.

"There are others too," I add. "I don't know if they'll help her... or try to take what she is."

The silence that follows is heavy with implications. With the understanding that whatever's coming, it's bigger than just us. Bigger than the sanctuary, than the Council, than anything we've prepared for.

I turn to Thane, meeting his silver gaze directly. "You know this too, don't you?"

Something shifts in his expression. A slow, sharp smile spreads across his lips, and for the first time since I've known him, it reaches his eyes.

"You're coming along nicely," he says, voice warm with what sounds like approval.

Heat crawls up my neck, but I don't look away. There's something in his tone, in the way he's watching me, that makes my pulse spike in ways I'm not ready to examine.

The moment stretches between us, charged with something I can't name.

Then Thane laughs.

It's the first real laugh I've heard from him. Not cold or cruel or mocking. Just... genuine. Rich and dark and entirely unexpected.

"Fuck," he says, shaking his head. "This is going to be a problem."

But he's still smiling when he says it.

And somehow, I get the feeling he wouldn't have it any other way.

Chapter 34
RHETT

Thane's laugh is still echoing in the room when we hear it.

A knock. Soft but insistent. Not at the front door—closer. Like someone's already inside the sanctuary.

We all go still at once, the easy moment evaporating like mist. Thane's expression shifts back to that controlled alertness, and Stellan straightens from his casual lean against the dresser.

"That's not forty-six minutes," Jace mutters, hand already moving toward his knives.

"No," Theo says quietly. "It's not."

We move as one toward the hallway, and that's when I see her.

Bree stands at the end of the corridor in an oversized hoodie—mine, I realize with a jolt—her dark hair a messy tangle around her shoulders. No shoes. Like she felt whatever's coming and moved on instinct alone.

The sight of her in my clothes does something to my chest. Something warm and possessive that I don't have time to examine.

"You felt it too," Theo says. Not a question.

She nods, wrapping her arms around herself. "Something's..." She pauses, looking toward the front of the sanctuary. "There are people here. A lot of people."

The knock comes again. Closer now. Like whoever it is has moved deeper into the sanctuary while we stood here talking.

"How many?" Thane asks, already moving past us toward the sound.

"I don't know." Bree's voice is small. "But they're not leaving."

That's when the first voice drifts through the walls. Then another. And another.

Not threatening. Not angry.

Reverent.

Fuck.

"They came for you," I say, the realization settling heavy in my stomach. "All of them."

Bree looks at me with those green eyes wide, and I see the exact moment she understands what this means. What she'll have to face.

"I can't—" she starts.

"You can," I say firmly, stepping closer. "But you don't have to do it alone."

The voices outside are getting louder. More confident. Like they know she's awake now, know she's listening.

"We should see what we're dealing with," Gray says, but his voice carries an edge that means he's already thinking strategy.

Wes hovers near Bree, not quite touching but close enough to catch her if she falls. The hunger that's been building in him seems muted now, replaced by something fiercer. More protective.

Stellan appears beside Thane, and for a moment they exchange one of those wordless communications that makes the rest of us feel like outsiders.

"They're not going away," Theo says quietly. "I can feel them settling in. Making camp."

Making themselves at home.

The knock comes a third time, and this time it's followed by a voice. Young. Female. Careful but insistent.

"We know you're awake. Please. We just want to talk."

Bree closes her eyes, takes a breath that shakes slightly on the exhale. When she opens them again, something has shifted. Not confidence exactly, but determination.

"Okay," she says. "Let's see what they want."

But as we start moving toward the front of the sanctuary, I catch the way her hands tremble slightly. The way she glances back at us like she's checking that we're still there.

And I make a decision.

Whatever happens next—whatever these people want from her—they're going to have to go through us first.

Because she might be the one they came for, but she's not the one who's going to face them alone.

Heat flickers under my skin, just for a moment. A promise. A warning.

Let them come.

We'll be ready.

The front door of the sanctuary opens to something that steals the breath from my lungs.

Dozens of them. Maybe a hundred. Spread across the sanctuary grounds like they've been waiting here for hours. Some kneeling on the pale stone paths. Some standing in loose clusters among the flowering trees. All of them watching the doorway.

Watching for her.

The numbers don't scare me. It's the intent that makes my jaw clench. People don't come in groups like this for protection. They come for possession.

Worship isn't love. And it's never safe.

The moment Bree steps into view beside me, a ripple moves through the crowd like wind over water. I watch faces change—hope bleeding into awe, awe sharpening into something hungrier. Calculation hiding behind reverence.

They're already rewriting her story and she hasn't even opened her mouth.

Bree takes a shaky breath, then steps forward. I catch the slight tremor in her hands before she clasps them together, but her voice carries clearly across the field.

"I don't know what this is yet," she says. "I don't know what any of this means. But if you're here because you need help... I'll try."

The honesty in her words hits me in the chest. Raw. Real. Everything they'll choose not to hear.

The crowd doesn't applaud. Instead, there's a moment of absolute silence. Then whispers. Reverent nods. The soft sound of more people dropping to their knees.

But as I scan the crowd again, looking for other threats, other presumptions, I catch something that makes me pause.

One face in the back. Tall, broad-shouldered, dark hair. While everyone else watches us—cataloguing, measuring, wanting—his attention is fixed entirely on Bree. And the expression on his face...

Relief. Raw and genuine, like he's been holding his breath for days and can finally exhale.

It's the only honest emotion in the entire crowd.

"We knew you'd come," a voice calls out—a woman somewhere in the middle of the crowd. "The Ether called us to you."

And that's when someone steps forward.

Not violently. Not threateningly. Just... presumptively. Like proximity to her is a right they've earned by showing up. They reach out—not quite touching, but close enough that intent is clear.

I move.

One deliberate step forward. Hands loose, posture calm, but my presence cuts through the space between them like a blade. I don't need fire. My body is the warning.

You don't touch what isn't yours.

The person stops. Steps back. Gets the message.

But as I scan the crowd again, looking for other threats, other presumptions, I catch something that makes my blood go cold.

One face. One expression.

Wrong.

Too still while everyone else shifts and murmurs. Too calm while Bree speaks again. And when she mentions trying to help, they smile.

Not relief. Not gratitude.

Anticipation.

That one's not here for sanctuary. That one's here for her.

I note the subtle shift around me—Stellan's attention sharpening on the same face, Gray edging closer to Bree's position, Thane's silver eyes flicking once in acknowledgment. He knows. But he says nothing.

The moment stretches, then breaks as Bree finishes speaking and starts to turn back toward the sanctuary. The crowd begins to move—not leaving, but settling. Finding places to linger. Making themselves comfortable.

Making themselves at home.

But it's not just the one wrong face I'm watching now. It's the others—the ones approaching Wes with shy smiles, the woman who brushes Theo's hand as she passes, the group that follows Jace's movement like he's their new favorite show.

I recognize it for what it is. Not connection. Just access.

They want the ones she stood beside. They think touching them means touching her.

Bree starts to head inside, unaware of the eyes that track her movement. Unaware of the way some of them are already looking at the rest of us like we're part of whatever they think they've found.

I don't follow her. Not yet.

Instead, I stay planted, watching the one who smiled. Watching how they catalogue every window, every door, every path. How they note which direction she went.

If Bree doesn't see it yet, I will. If she doesn't stop it, I will.

The heat under my skin flares, just once. A reminder of what I could do. What I would do, if it comes to that.

They think standing on this land makes them part of her. They're wrong.

Because she doesn't belong to the Ether. She belongs to herself.

And I will burn down anyone who forgets that.

Chapter 35
THANE

Bree walks ahead of the group as we file back into the sanctuary, wrapped in silence that feels more like armor than quiet. Her bare feet make no sound on the stone floor, but I can feel the tension radiating off her in waves.

She doesn't speak. But I can feel her pulse from here. Fast. Controlled. Pretending to be fine.

She touched me in front of them all. And now they think she's made a choice.

Behind her, the others process what just happened in their own ways.

"That one with the gold cuffs?" Jace says, grin sharp and cocky. "Definitely wanted to climb me like a tree."

"Here we go," Wes mutters, but there's no real annoyance in it.

"I mean, who wouldn't?" Jace continues, spreading his arms wide. "It's the Ether effect. We're glowing, boys."

"They're not drawn to you," Theo says quietly. "They're drawn to her."

The correction lands like a stone in still water. Jace's grin falters slightly, but he doesn't argue.

Gray doesn't speak at all. He's tracking the perimeter through the windows, watching for movement. Watching for the wrong one Rhett noticed.

Bree doesn't react. Doesn't turn. Doesn't flinch.

But her heart stutters. Just once.

I hear it. A slight hitch in the rhythm of her pulse—so fast, so careful—and for anyone else, it would seem unchanged. But not to me.

She heard them. All of it. And she's locking it down so hard the tension tightens the air.

They think she's walking ahead because she's strong.

But I know the truth. She's walking ahead so they won't see her break.

Pain flares beneath my ribs. Not from the knowledge of what's happening to Bree right now.

I'm being summoned.

But this isn't the usual Council summons—sharp and demanding. This slides under my skin like silk laced with venom. Quieter. Curated.

Personal.

Nyx.

I stumble slightly, catch myself against the wall. The others notice—I see Stellan's head turn, Rhett's attention sharpen—but I wave them off.

"Council business," I manage. "I'll be back."

Before anyone can respond, the magic takes me.

I don't appear in the formal Council chamber.

Fuck.

This is Nyx's private domain—all velvet shadows and glowing orbs of light, reflective black floors that mirror everything twice. Opulent in a way that makes my skin crawl. She lounges on a throne that looks more like a bed, draped in silk that shifts color with her mood.

She's watching me with those predator eyes as she stands, making her way toward me, and I know immediately that this isn't going to be a simple interrogation.

"Thane," she purrs, rising with liquid grace. "You look... rattled."

"I look exactly as I always do."

She circles me, slow and deliberate. "Do you? Because the footage I've been seeing suggests otherwise."

My blood goes cold. "Footage?"

"Oh yes. It's everywhere now. EtherTube, magical news feeds, private Council surveillance." Her smile is all teeth. "The moment she touched you. The way you didn't flinch. The way you looked at her like she was the only thing in the world that mattered."

She stops directly in front of me, close enough that I can smell the magic rolling off her skin. Dangerous. Intoxicating.

"She touched you first," Nyx continues, voice dropping to something almost intimate. "And you didn't flinch. Didn't pull away. Didn't maintain the distance we all know you're so good at."

"It was strategic."

"Was it?" She reaches out, trails one finger along my jaw. "Because it looked like surrender to me."

I don't move. Don't react. "Everything I do serves the Council's interests."

"Of course it does." But her tone suggests she doesn't believe me for a second. "Tell me, Thane—when you bled for her, when she chose to use the Ether on you instead of letting you suffer, what did you feel?"

"Nothing."

"Liar." The word is soft, almost affectionate. "You felt chosen. You felt wanted. You felt like maybe, for the first time in centuries, someone saw you as more than just a useful monster."

Her hand moves to my chest, palm flat over where my heart should be racing. I keep it steady through will alone.

"Are you hers now, Thane?" she asks. "Or are you still mine to play with?"

The question hangs between us, loaded with implications I'm not ready to face. Because the answer should be simple. Should be automatic.

But it's not.

"I serve the Council," I say instead. "I serve the mission. Let them see her. Let them fear her. I'll keep her public. Manageable. The more visible she is, the easier it'll be to control her."

Nyx studies my face for a long moment, and I can see her weighing my words against what she knows. What she's observed.

Finally, she steps back. "Very well. But Thane?" Her smile turns sharp. "Try not to look so eager the next time you bleed for her. It's becoming a bit obvious."

Before I can respond, the magic yanks me sideways again.

The formal Council chamber materializes around me, and I'm not surprised to find the others already there. Valdris paces near her throne, flames licking at her heels. Marcus sits rigid in his chair, expression cold as winter. Eris leans forward, silver eyes blank with prophecy.

And Nyx, already seated, watches me with that knowing smile.

"You were touched," Valdris says without preamble. "The world saw it."

"Are you compromised?" Marcus adds, voice sharp with suspicion.

I take my seat—last in the circle, slightly back, lower than the others—and meet their stares with practiced calm.

"No," I say evenly. "I'm focused."

I pause knowing.

"And I have a proposal."

That gets their attention. Valdris's flames flicker higher. "Explain."

"We can't control what people felt when they saw her. Or what they think they saw when she reached for me. The narrative is already moving—and trying to crush it will only make it stronger."

I pause. Let that settle.

"But if we let her stay visible, if we make her familiar—marketable, even—then she becomes a symbol. And symbols can be managed. Stories can be rewritten."

Nyx leans forward, interested now.

"I'll feed the right leaks. Whispers of instability. Of hunger. Of a girl in over her head. If the public starts to fear her, we don't have to. They'll do the work for us."

I look directly at Marcus. "Visibility is vulnerability. And the more she shines, the easier it'll be to gut her—if we decide we need to."

"She's untrained. Emotional. The more visible she becomes, the more she'll rely on public approval. The more she needs to be seen as benevolent." I pause again, letting them follow the logic. "It makes her controllable. Predictable. She won't risk anything that might turn them against her."

Marcus leans forward, interested despite himself. "And you'll monitor this... how?"

"I'll stay close. Report everything. Guide her choices when possible." The lies flow easier now. "Let her think she's choosing her own path while we direct where it leads."

"And if she becomes too powerful?" Valdris asks.

"Then we know exactly where to find her. And everyone will be watching when we act."

They exchange looks—the kind of silent communication that means they're weighing the proposal.

"It has merit," Marcus admits grudgingly.

"The visibility aspect is sound," Valdris agrees. "Better to know where she is than let her disappear into hiding."

Eris speaks, her voice carrying that otherworldly quality. "Your thread was faint before. It's not anymore. It burns silver now. Bright enough to see from the Veil itself."

Something cold settles in my stomach, but I keep my expression neutral. "Then you know exactly where my loyalties lie."

"Do we?" Marcus challenges. "Because from where I sit, it looks like you've developed an attachment."

"I've developed an investment," I correct. "She's powerful. She's going to reshape everything. I intend to be on the winning side when she does."

The lie tastes familiar by now. Comfortable.

"Very well," Nyx says finally, speaking for the group. "We approve your strategy. Keep her visible. Keep her manageable. But Thane?" Her eyes lock with mine. "Don't make the mistake of thinking we can't see the difference between duty and desire."

The dismissal is clear. The magic begins to pull at me again, preparing to send me back.

"One more thing," Eris calls out as I start to fade. "The next time she touches you? She'll leave more than just a handprint. She'll leave a piece of herself. And you'll take it willingly."

I reappear in the sanctuary hallway, legs unsteady for just a moment before I catch myself. The familiar weight of the building settles around me, grounding me in something that feels more real than Council chambers and power games.

Stellan is waiting, leaning against the wall with that knowing expression of his.

"That bad?" he asks.

"They believe what they need to."

"Which is?"

"That I'm the leash."

His mouth curves slightly. "And what are you really?"

I pause, the words sticking in my throat. Because for the first time in centuries, I know the answer.

"Already tethered," I say finally.

Stellan's smile widens. "Thought so."

He pushes off from the wall, starts walking toward the main hall where I can hear voices—the others processing what happened outside, probably planning next moves.

"Coming?" he asks over his shoulder.

I take a breath, square my shoulders, and follow him toward whatever comes next.

But Eris's words echo in my mind with every step: *The next time she touches you, she'll leave a piece of herself. And you'll take it willingly.*

The worst part?

I already know she's right.

Chapter 36
BREE

I slip out through the back door and don't tell anyone where I'm going.

The quiet hits like cold water. No voices. No eyes. Just me and the early morning air and grass that's wet against my bare feet.

I should put shoes on. I should go back inside and pretend everything's fine.

Instead, I keep walking.

"That one with the gold cuffs? Definitely wanted to climb me like a tree."

Jace's voice won't leave my head. All cocky and amused, like it was *funny*. Like watching strangers want them was some kind of joke.

I stop walking. My hands are shaking.

They didn't look at me. Not once. Not when that woman brushed Theo's hand or when people started following Jace with their eyes. They just... talked. Laughed. Made jokes about being wanted.

And I stood there listening, feeling something ugly twist in my chest.

"They're not mine," I whisper to the empty garden.

But the words taste wrong.

Because maybe I don't own them, but I thought... I don't know what I thought. That they'd at least notice I was there? That someone would ask if I was okay with watching strangers reach for them like they had the right?

I wrap Rhett's hoodie tighter around me and start walking again, following the stone path through the trees. Everything here is soft and glowing and peaceful, but all I can think about is the sound of Jace's laugh. The way none of them turned around.

The way they talked about being wanted like it was just another Tuesday.

I've never been wanted. Not really. Not in a way that didn't come with conditions or expectations or someone trying to use me for something.

But watching them get that attention—attention that only existed because they stood next to me—made something in me hurt. Something I don't have words for.

Maybe it would've been easier if they'd actually done something. Kissed someone. Flirted back. That would've been clear.

But this? This felt like watching them discover they could have anyone they wanted. Because of magic I didn't mean to give them.

Magic that made them glow, apparently.

I think about leaving. It wouldn't be hard. Pack the few things I have, walk away before anyone notices I'm gone. It's what I've always done when things got complicated.

You disappear before they notice you're breaking.

That was Theo. Calling me out. Seeing through me when I thought I was being careful.

And here I am again, walking alone, thinking about running.

"I'm still here," I say out loud, because maybe if I say it enough times, I'll believe it.

The ground pulses under my feet.

Not scary. Not demanding. Just... awake. Like the Ether heard me and decided to pay attention.

I look up, and suddenly I can feel them. All the people camped beyond the garden. Families sleeping on the ground. Kids curled up in tents that aren't warm enough. Strangers who followed something they felt without knowing what they'd find.

They came here because of me. Because of what I am.

And they're sleeping on dirt.

I take a step forward, then another, until I'm standing at the edge of where the garden meets the forest.

The Ether stirs. Waiting.

I don't know what I'm doing. I just know I can't let this be what I offer people. Cold ground and rough camping and nothing else.

I step across the line.

Everything changes.

Trees bend without breaking, branches weaving together like they're dancing. Moss rises from the ground, soft and glowing, forming walls that feel alive. Leaves press and shape themselves into roofs that let in just enough starlight.

The forest doesn't become something else. It just... opens. Makes room.

Dozens of small homes bloom into existence. Then more. Each one different, shaped by need and comfort and something deeper than just shelter.

I stand in the middle of it all, watching the Ether work without me telling it what to do. It knows what people need. Knows how to help.

For the first time today, I feel like I did something right.

Something that matters.

I'm still staring at the glowing moss walls when I feel eyes on me.

Just... watching.

I turn, expecting maybe Rhett or Gray, someone who noticed I was gone.

Instead, there's a stranger standing at the edge of the light. Tall, dark hair, wearing clothes that look like he's been traveling. There's a scar visible above his collar, and his eyes are the color of burnt honey.

He's not looking at me like the crowd did. Not like I'm something powerful or dangerous or useful.

He's looking at me like he wants me.

The thought should scare me.

But it doesn't.

Instead, something warm unfurls in my chest. Something I've never felt before and don't have a name for.

"You didn't have to do that for them," he says. His voice is low, careful.

"I know."

He takes a step closer, and I don't move away. The way he looks at me makes my skin feel warm, makes me notice things I usually don't. Like how his eyes track the curve of my face. How his attention feels different from the reverent stares I've been getting.

This isn't awe. This is interest. Personal, male interest.

And I like it.

The realization hits me like a shock. I should be cautious. Should ask more questions, demand explanations.

Instead, I find myself wondering what his hands would feel like. What his voice sounds like when it's not being careful.

"Who are you?" I ask.

His mouth curves into something that's not quite a smile. Dangerous, maybe, but not unkind.

"Call me Seth."

The name settles somewhere under my ribs like heat that won't leave.

I don't trust him. Don't know him. Don't know why he's here or what he wants.

But for the first time in my life, I want to be wanted. Not for what I can do or fix or heal, but just... for me.

And I'm not going to apologize for that.

Chapter 37
WES

The crowd's gone, but I can still feel their hands on my skin—not the actual touches, but the memory of them. The way that woman brushed my arm like she had a right to. The way that man's eyes lingered like I was something he could take home. The hunger had spiked sharp and immediate when it happened, not from wanting them but from them wanting me, and it left me feeling scraped raw and empty in a way that has nothing to do with satisfaction.

I'm standing in the main hallway now, watching Rhett check the windows for the third time while Gray goes quiet in that calculating way that means he's tracking threats. Jace has gone quiet too, the swagger from earlier completely gone, and I can see the shame in the way he keeps running his hand through his hair like he's trying to scrub away what he said.

"That one with the gold cuffs? Definitely wanted to climb me like a tree."

The words echo in my head, all cockiness and casual dismissal, like it was funny instead of wrong. Like watching strangers reach for us was just another Tuesday instead of something that made my skin crawl.

But what makes it worse—what makes the shame burn hot behind my ribs—is that no one's asking where Bree went.

I felt it the second she slipped away. Like a note went missing in a song only I could hear. But I didn't follow. Didn't speak up. Didn't do anything except stand here listening to Jace joke about being wanted while the only person whose attention I actually crave right now disappeared into the gardens.

She probably just needs space, I tell myself, but the lie tastes stale even in my own mind.

Because I remember the exact moment it happened—the way she stepped back when the crowd pressed closer, the way her face went carefully blank when that woman touched my arm. She saw everything. Heard Jace laugh about it. Watched us all treat it like entertainment instead of violation.

And I let her.

I need to get out of this hallway, away from their voices and their easy dismissal of what just happened. Away from the way none of them seem to notice that the most important person in the room has vanished. I retreat to my bedroom, close the door, and lean against it like it might keep the shame from seeping in through the cracks.

The hunger gnaws at my ribs, sharper tonight than it's been in days. Like it's feeding on my guilt instead of fading, growing stronger with every breath I take that doesn't include her presence to ground me.

I remember the way she looked at me when she found me in the attic that afternoon—not curious or afraid, just... present. Like my company was enough. Like I was still just Wes.

But that was before the hunger started gnawing at the edges. Before I started hiding it. Before Gray noticed. Before Stellan stepped in like he already knew what I was becoming.

She doesn't know what I am. Not really. Not yet.

She never looked at me like she was afraid—but that's only because I've made sure she never had a reason to.

And that's the part I can't breathe around. Not the hunger. Not the magic. The possibility that the moment she does see it—see me—she'll pull away.

And tonight I let strangers treat me like a prize while she watched from the sidelines.

A knock at my door interrupts the spiral. I expect Jace, maybe Theo coming to check on everyone. Instead, it's Stellan leaning against the doorframe with his arms crossed, expression serious in a way that makes my stomach drop.

"You smell like panic," he says without preamble.

"Thanks for the pep talk," I mutter, but he's already stepping into the room without an invitation, closing the door behind him with that grace of his that already makes the space feel smaller.

"Breathe slower," he says, voice calm but firm. "Feed later. Or not at all. But don't lie to yourself about what this is."

"Easy for you to say." The words come out sharper than I intended, raw with frustration I've been swallowing for weeks. "You've had centuries to figure out control. I've had two weeks and a target painted on my back by magic I didn't ask for."

"She's not a target," Stellan says, and something in his tone makes me go still. "She's a mirror."

"What's that supposed to mean?"

He steps closer—not seductive, not feeding, just present in that unnerving way that makes it impossible to hide behind deflection.

"What do you want, Wes?"

The question hangs between us, loaded with implications I'm not ready to face. I think about deflecting, making a joke, brushing this off like I always do when things get too real. But the hunger is clawing at my chest and Stellan's steady gaze won't let me retreat into comfortable lies.

"I want her to look at me like she used to," I admit, the words scraping my throat raw. "Before I became something she has to worry about."

Stellan studies my face for a long moment, then steps back with something that might be approval flickering in his expression.

"You're not dangerous to her," he says quietly. "You're dangerous to yourself. Decide which one matters more."

He moves toward the door, pauses with his hand on the handle.

"Figure it out—before she realizes someone already has."

Then he's gone, leaving me alone with the weight of his words and the ache that won't fade no matter how I try to breathe through it.

I sink onto the edge of my bed, chest heaving with the effort of keeping myself together. The hunger hasn't faded—if anything, it's sharper now, more focused—but the noise in my head has shifted from panic to something that feels almost like clarity.

I think about the way Bree said my name that time in the attic, soft and careful like it mattered. The way her presence grounds me even when everything else feels like it's spinning out of control. The way she sees me as Wes instead of whatever I'm becoming, like the person I've always been is worth preserving even as magic reshapes me into something I don't recognize.

And I let today make me forget that. Let strangers' attention distract me from the one of the only people whose opinions actually count.

If she doesn't come back, it'll be because I didn't try hard enough to make her want to stay.

I can't let that happen.

Chapter 38
BREE

I slip back through the garden door and my hands are shaking.

I don't know why. Don't know what just happened out there or why my chest feels tight and warm and wrong all at once.

The hallway stretches out empty in front of me. Everyone's probably dealing with whatever this morning was—the crowd, the speech, all those eyes. My bare feet are silent on the stone, and there are leaves stuck to my legs from walking through the forest.

Rhett's hoodie still smells like him. Safe. Familiar.

But I don't feel safe.

I keep hearing Seth's voice. The way he said his name.

Call me Seth.

And those eyes. Dark gold and interested and looking at me like—

I shake my head. Try to focus on walking. On getting to my room. On not thinking about the way my pulse spiked when he smiled.

I round the corner and freeze.

Wes is standing at the end of the hallway.

Just standing there. Like he's been waiting.

My stomach does something complicated.

I look down, try to walk past him without making eye contact. Maybe he won't—

"Bree."

I don't stop.

"Bree, please."

My feet keep moving, but something in his voice makes my chest ache. "I can't," I whisper.

I take a breath thinking I'll make it past him.

"Dammit, Bree."

I stop. My hand finds the door handle, grips it hard.

I can hear him moving behind me. Slow footsteps. Careful.

"I know you heard us," he says quietly. "What Jace said. How we... how I let it happen."

The Ether starts curling around my ankles. I don't call it. It just comes. And it's reaching for him.

"What is it doing?" Wes sounds confused. Maybe a little scared.

I don't know. I never know what the Ether's doing until it's already done it.

The Ether touches him—wraps around his arm, brushes his face. And something happens.

His shoulders drop. His breathing changes. Like whatever's been eating at him just... eased.

When I finally turn around, his eyes look different. Open. Like the Wes I remember before everything got complicated.

"I saw the way they looked at you," I say. The words just come out.

He shakes his head. "I didn't want them."

"I know." My throat feels tight. "But I hated it anyway."

He takes a step closer. Not touching. Just closer.

"Why?" His voice is soft.

I don't know how to answer that. Don't understand the ugly feeling that twisted in my chest when that woman touched his arm. When people started following him with their eyes like he was something they could have.

"I don't know," I admit. "It just felt wrong. Like they didn't... like you weren't..."

"What?"

I step closer. Look up at him. His pupils are wide and dark and I can feel the heat coming off his skin.

The words are right there. Waiting. And I know I shouldn't say them.

"It felt like you were mine," I whisper.

I shouldn't say that. But it's true.

The words surprise me anyway. I didn't mean to say them. Didn't even know I was thinking them.

But they're true.

"If you don't want this," he says carefully, "stop me now."

My heart is beating so fast I can hear it in my ears. I reach up, touch his face. His skin is warm and real and right there.

"Then don't make me decide."

He kisses me.

And it's nothing like I expected. Nothing like the careful, gentle way people have touched me before. This is desperate and hungry and it makes something in my chest crack open and bleed and heal all at once.

His mouth moves against mine like he's been starving for this, like I'm the only thing that can fill the emptiness inside him. I gasp against his lips and he deepens the kiss, one hand tangling in my hair while the other presses against my lower back, pulling me closer until there's no space left between us.

I feel it as the Ether explodes around us, silver and bright and celebrating, wrapping us in light that makes everything feel sacred. I can taste his need, his relief, his hunger finally finding something that feeds it instead of hollowing him out.

My fingers fist in his shirt and I pull him down to me, wanting more, needing more. He responds by pressing me back against the door, his body warm and solid and perfect against mine. When his teeth graze my bottom lip, I make a sound I've never made before—desperate and wanting and completely his.

This is what was missing in the forest. This recognition. This feeling of coming home to something I didn't know I'd lost.

This is Wes.

My Wes.

He kisses me like he's trying to memorize the taste of me, like he's afraid I'll disappear if he stops. His thumb traces the line of my jaw and I shiver, pressing closer, wanting to crawl inside his skin and live there.

When we break apart, I can't breathe. My lips feel swollen and my whole body is buzzing and he's looking at me like I'm something precious.

"You didn't hurt me," I whisper.

"I can't," he says back. "Not with you."

We just stand there for a minute, breathing. The Ether settles around our feet, quiet now.

I touch his cheek one more time. Then I reach for the door handle.

"Good morning, Wes."

He doesn't try to follow. Just watches as I slip inside and close the door.

I lean against it, heart still racing, fingers pressed to my mouth.

I can still taste him.

And for the first time since this whole thing started, I think I might know what I want.

Chapter 39
BREE

I'm sitting on my bed, fingers still pressed to my lips when the knock comes. I can still taste him. Still feel the press of his mouth against mine, the way his hands threaded through my hair. My whole body is buzzing, lit up from the inside.

I've kissed others. I've been kissed with tenderness, with care, even with longing. And every one of those moments mattered. They made me feel safe. Chosen. *Seen.*

But this was different.

This time, it wasn't just about being wanted.

It was about *wanting back.*

And for the first time in my life, I didn't feel the need to shrink from that. I didn't feel ashamed of it. I just... *felt.* All of it. And I still do.

My lips still tingle. My heart hasn't stopped pounding. But what scares me most isn't what just happened.

It's how much I didn't want to run from it.

The knock comes again, soft and hesitant.

"Come in," I call, expecting maybe Theo or Rhett checking on me.

Instead, it's Mairen. The woman cooking not just for us, but the entire crowd of people who have come be. She's holding a small lantern, and her expression is somewhere between sheepish and hopeful.

"I'm sorry to bother you," she says, voice trembling slightly. "But I tho ught... well, I set something up. For dinner. And I was hoping you might join us."

I blink, confused. "Us?"

"All of you," she clarifies, then looks down at her hands. "I know this morning was... a lot. And I thought maybe you'd all like somewhere quiet to just... breathe for a while"

There's something in her voice that makes my chest tight. Like this matters to her. Like she's offering something precious.

"What did you set up?" I ask.

Her face brightens. "Come see?"

She holds out her hand, and after a moment's hesitation, I take it.

***

The garden takes my breath away.

The sun is setting, painting everything in gold and amber, and the Ether is awake but gentle—soft curls of mist threading through the grass like silk. But that's not what stops me cold.

Floating orbs of warm light hover above a long, low table like captured fireflies. Bioluminescent flowers I've never seen before sway in the evening breeze, casting everything in a soft, otherworldly glow. The table is sur- rounded by cushions and blankets, with food laid out that smells like comfort and home.

It's beautiful. Intimate. Perfect.

And clearly arranged for us.

"Mairen," I whisper. "This is..."

She guides me to a cushion at the head of the table, then kneels beside me. Her eyes are bright with unshed tears.

"Thank you," she says, voice thick with emotion. "Not just for the sanctuary. For the home you built without even meaning to."

I don't understand. "What home?"

"The houses," she says, gesturing toward the forest edge. "The ones that grew when you walked through the trees this morning. My friend Kira—she's been traveling for weeks, sleeping rough, caring for her baby girl alone. And the house you made for her..." She wipes her eyes. "It was exactly what she needed. Like you saw her without even meeting her. Like you made her feel chosen."

My throat goes tight. "I didn't even know she was there."

"That's what makes it beautiful," Mairen says softly. "You didn't do it for credit or recognition. You just... cared. And it shows."

Before I can respond, footsteps approach from behind us. I turn to see the others stepping into the garden one by one.

Rhett stiffens first, eyes scanning the floating lights like he's checking for threats. Wes looks directly at me, something soft and uncertain in his expression. Gray notices the bioluminescent flowers with quiet appreciation. Jace just stops and stares, mouth slightly open. Theo whispers, "What is this?"

Thane and Stellan follow behind them, both taking in the scene with different kinds of surprise.

I open my mouth to explain, but Mairen speaks first.

"She made it for you," she says simply. "All of you. For us."

Rhett frowns. "Made what?"

Mairen gestures toward the forest. "The houses. The safe spaces. The way people are gathering without fear." Her voice grows stronger. "We didn't even have to knock. The doors just opened. Like she knew what we needed before we did."

The silence that follows is heavy with something I can't name.

"Come," Mairen says, rising from her knees. "Eat. Talk. Just... be together."

We settle around the table in a quiet that feels sacred instead of awkward. The food is warm and perfect, and the floating lights cast everything in a gentle glow that makes even the sharp edges feel softer.

For a while, no one speaks. We just eat, lost in our own thoughts.

Then Jace clears his throat.

"I fucked up this morning," he says quietly. "What I said—the way I talked about it like it was funny. I shouldn't have. I always make it a joke when I don't know how to handle whatever is happening." He looks directly at me. "But you were right there, and I didn't think. I'm sorry."

Rhett sets down his fork. "I noticed something was wrong. Could see it in the way you stepped back, went quiet. But I didn't say anything because I wasn't sure it was my place." He pauses. "Now I know it always is. When it comes to you."

Gray's voice is quiet when he speaks. "I saw you walk away. I should have gone after you."

"I should've stopped Jace," Theo adds. "I didn't. And that's on me too."

Wes is quiet for a long moment, then looks up. "I let myself be wanted by people I don't care about... and let the person who matters walk away."

The admission hangs in the air between us, weighted with everything that happened in the hallway.

Then, surprisingly, Thane speaks.

"You disappeared," he says, silver eyes finding mine. "And I noticed. I just didn't know what I was allowed to do about it."

Stellan adds softly, "That's the problem. None of us are asking. We're all assuming. And it's starting to show."

I stare around the table at all of them—these men who've somehow become the center of my world without me noticing. They're not perfect. They mess up, make assumptions, hurt each other without meaning to.

But they're here. They're trying.

And maybe that's enough.

"I don't know how to do this," I admit quietly. "Any of this. I don't know how to be wanted or needed or... important to people. I've never had that before."

"None of us do," Rhett says. "But we figure it out as we go."

"Together," Wes adds, and something warm unfurls in my chest.

The Ether curls gently around our feet, content and settled in a way it hasn't been in days. Like it approves of this moment, this honesty, this decision to stay instead of run.

We finish dinner in comfortable quiet, the floating lights growing brighter as true darkness falls. No one moves to leave. No one breaks the silence with jokes or deflection.

We just... stay.

And for the first time in too long, staying doesn't feel like a trap.

It feels like a promise.

Chapter 40
JACE

"You seriously want to go alone again?"

Bree pauses in the doorway, one hand on the frame, and gives me that look. The one that says she knows exactly what I'm doing but hasn't decided if she's annoyed or amused yet.

It's the fourth day in a row she's done this—slipping out after breakfast to check on the camps, help with repairs, heal small things with that instinctive Ether touch of hers. And it's the fourth day I've watched her go without saying anything.

"Come on, sunshine," I continue, leaning against the wall with what I hope looks like casual confidence. "You've got, like, ten adoring body-guards and you pick 'solo brooding in the woods' as your hobby?"

"Jace..." There's warning in her voice, but her mouth is fighting a smile.

I grin. "Tell me you don't want me with you. Go ahead. Say it with a straight face."

She tries. I can see her trying to look stern, trying to maintain that careful distance she's been wrapping around herself lately. But the smile wins, small and genuine, and something warm settles in my chest.

"Fine," she says. "But no complaining when your shoes get muddy."

"Sweetheart, I live for muddy shoes."

She rolls her eyes as we head out through the back door, as I pretend not to notice.

The sanctuary forest is alive with dappled sunlight and the soft hum of Ether-touched homes scattered between the trees like living lanterns. It's been a few days since the garden dinner, since everything shifted and settled into something that feels almost normal.

Well. Normal for us.

Bree moves through the camps with easy grace, checking on new arrivals, offering help in that way that only Bree can manage. The Ether flows around her feet like water, lighting her steps, responding to needs she hasn't even noticed yet.

A teenage girl braiding flowers into the moss-covered steps of her new home looks up as we pass. She holds out a white blossom to Bree with shy reverence.

"For you, Miss Ether."

I snort. "That's not a name, that's a superhero alias."

Bree takes the flower anyway, touches the girl's hand gently. "Thank you. It's beautiful."

We keep walking, past a mother waving from her doorway as Bree adjusts a fallen branch with a gesture. Past an elderly man tending a garden that definitely wasn't there yesterday. Everyone we pass smiles when they see her. Real smiles. The kind that come from gratitude and genuine affection.

And watching her respond to them—shy but warm, giving pieces of herself without thinking—makes something in my chest feel too tight.

I'm proud of her. Proud to be walking beside her. Proud that she chose to let me come along.

But there's something else underneath that I'm not sure I can think about right now.

A group of kids spots us and comes running, eyes bright with excitement.

"Are you the one with the flying knives?" one of them asks, bouncing on his toes.

I grin, pulling a blade from my belt and spinning it on my finger. The kids gasp appropriately, and I show off just enough to earn some impressed whispers before making the knife disappear again.

"Magic," I say with a wink.

Bree's watching me with something soft in her expression. "Show-off."

"Always."

We're still laughing when Bree suddenly stops walking.

Like full-stop, mid-step, air sucked out of the moment.

Her whole posture changes—shoulders tensing, breath catching, head tilted slightly like she's just seen something impossible.

I follow her line of sight.

There's a guy up ahead. Tall. Broad shoulders. Rolled sleeves. He's on a ladder, securing a moss-woven beam for one of the new houses. Moving like he belongs there. Like he's done this a thousand times. Confident. Capable. Maybe a little too capable.

I've never seen him before in my life.

Bree stares at him like she has.

She takes a step forward, then another. Her voice is barely above a whisper. "Seth?"

And just like that, I know exactly how absolutely fucked I am.

Because I've never heard her say my name like that.

The guy—Seth, apparently—looks down and sees her. And his whole face softens, like she's exactly who he was hoping to find.

He climbs down slow, steady, measured. Like he's had practice making people feel safe. Like he's *good* at it.

When he reaches the ground, he doesn't look at me. Doesn't look around. He just looks at her.

"Bree," he says, and it's not just a name. It's an entire sentence. A memory. A promise.

And maybe I'm imagining it, but she sways toward him like her body forgot I was even standing here.

I step forward, throwing on a grin that feels like armor. "Hey there. You new in town?"

He extends his hand. "Seth."

"He helped one of the families near the border yesterday morning," Bree explains, and I can hear the soft pleasure in her voice. "Stayed behind after the walk. I told him it was okay."

Of course she did.

I shake his hand, grip firm enough to make a point. "Of course it's okay. She's the queen of the glowing forest now. You need a crown? We can probably whip one up out of moonbeams."

Seth grins, and it's annoyingly genuine. "You must be one of hers."

The words hits somewhere inside me I didn't know existed.

One of hers.

He's not wrong. But hearing it said out loud, so casually, makes something in me twist with heat.

I liked it better before it meant competition.

Bree doesn't notice the tension. She's too busy asking Seth how his morning went, if he needs anything. When he says he's fine, she smiles—not the ethereal, magic-touched smile she gives the crowds, but the real one. The shy one she gave me once when I bandaged her ankle last fall.

And it's not mine this time.

We leave Seth with the family and continue our rounds, but something's shifted. I've gone quiet, and for once, I can't find a joke to fill the silence.

Bree glances at me after a few minutes. "You okay?"

I try to brush it off, make some crack about Seth needing a haircut. But the words feel hollow even as I say them.

Because the truth is, I didn't think it would feel like this. Watching her look at someone else the way she looked at him. Not when she's still looking at all of us too.

I wasn't ready for him or anyone else to matter. Not to her. Not like this.

"Jace?" She's stopped walking, concern clear in her green eyes.

"I'm fine, sweetheart," I say, but even I can hear how thin it sounds.

She studies my face for a moment, then calls something over her shoulder about checking on the family by the creek. I watch the curve of her spine as she walks ahead, the sway of her hair catching sunlight.

I don't follow right away.

Because standing here, watching her move through the world like she belongs in it, I'm realizing something I should have figured out weeks ago.

If I want to be someone she chooses—really chooses, not just tolerates or finds amusing—I've got to stop pretending I don't care if she doesn't.

I've got to stop hiding behind jokes and sharp grins and casual indifference.

I've got to let it matter.

Finally, I start walking again, catching up to her easy stride. But something in me has shifted, settled into a new shape.

I'm not sure if that scares me or excites me more. I guess we'll find out.

Chapter 41
THANE

I've been pacing this hallway for twenty minutes.

Waiting. Like some lovesick fool instead of a centuries-old vampire with better things to do than track the movements of one untrained Source.

It's been three days since the Council summons, since I was yanked away from her when everything started shifting. Three days of watching her slip out each morning to tend to the camps, and three days of feeling her absence like a missing tooth I can't stop probing with my tongue.

Blocking the corridor like a territorial animal.

Pathetic.

The sound of footsteps makes me go still. Light, familiar, accompanied by the soft whisper of Ether that always announces her presence. I should move. Should pretend I was just passing through.

Instead, I plant myself more firmly in the center of the hallway.

She rounds the corner and nearly walks into me, pulling up short with surprise that quickly shifts to wariness.

"You're blocking the hallway," she says.

The simple observation carries an edge that wasn't there before. Good. She's learning not to back down.

"You've been gone a long time."

The words come out more accusatory than I intended. More possessive. I watch her shoulders stiffen, see the exact moment her defenses go up.

"I was walking. Helping people."

With him. The thought burns through me before I can stop it. Because I know she wasn't alone today. Stellan mentioned seeing her with Jace this morning, and the scent of unfamiliar magic still clings to her hoodie.

Male magic. Not one of theirs.

"Helping." I let the word carry all my skepticism. "They'd kneel if you asked them to."

Her green eyes flash. "I didn't ask them to."

"No. But you didn't stop them either."

It's cruel, and I know it. But watching her flinch feels better than acknowledging the real reason I'm standing here like a jealous fool.

"Should I have?" Her voice sharpens, gains strength. "Should I tell them not to be grateful? Not to hope for something better?"

The fire in her tone does something to my chest. Makes me want to push harder, see how bright she can burn.

But then she hits me where I'm not prepared for it.

"You disappeared," she says suddenly. "After the crowd. After they all started looking at the others like... and then you were just gone."

The accusation lands and I feel like I'm gasping for air. I remember that moment—the Council summons hitting me like a brand beneath my ribs, yanking me away from her right when the attention on the others was making everything complicated.

"The Council summoned me," I say carefully.

"Of course they did." Bitterness, low and familiar. "Right when things got difficult."

I don't answer. Can't explain that leaving her that day felt like choosing duty over something I was only beginning to understand I wanted.

"You wouldn't understand."

"Try me."

I hesitate, almost looking pained. Because how do I explain centuries of conditioning? How do I tell her that every instinct I have says to protect the mission, serve the Council, maintain control—but all of that crumbles when she looks at me like I matter?

She flinches at my silence, and I hate myself for it.

"No," she says quietly. "I suppose I wouldn't."

The admission in her voice—hurt, confusion, something that might be disappointment—makes my carefully constructed walls crack.

"You keep telling people you volunteered to find me because I was dangerous," she continues, stepping closer. Close enough that I can smell the forest in her hair, the lingering sweetness of her skin. "But you've never looked at me like I'm dangerous. Not once."

She's right. From the moment I first saw her, standing in that kitchen with mist curling around her feet, I've never looked at her and seen a threat.

I've looked at her and seen everything I thought I'd forgotten how to want.

"No."

"Then why—"

"But I have looked at you like you might ruin me."

The words tear out of me before I can stop them. Raw and honest in a way I haven't been with anyone in centuries. Her eyes widen, lips parting in surprise.

For a moment, we just stare at each other. The hallway feels charged, electric with possibility and fear.

Then she finds her voice, and it's stronger than I expected.

"If you're waiting for me to belong to someone, it's not going to be you who decides that."

She brushes past me, shoulder barely grazing my arm.

And everything changes.

The Ether rises from her skin like liquid silver, wrapping around me with deliberate intent. Not the chaotic hunger I've seen it display before, but something purposeful. But this time, it doesn't curl hungrily. It waits. Watches. Then chooses. Claiming.

It curls along my jaw, threads through my hair, settles against my chest like it recognizes something there. Like it's marking territory.

And it's not the first time.

I remember the attic. The door with the sigil that bloomed under her touch. The way the Ether had reached for me then too, tentative but present. She'd been so focused on the mark, on what it meant, that she hadn't noticed the mist threading toward me. Hadn't seen the way it tested the space between us.

But I had noticed. Had felt the electric pull of recognition.

I go completely still. Not from fear, but from the overwhelming right-ness of it.

This isn't random magic responding to proximity. This is choice. Recognition. The Ether claiming me as surely as if she'd pressed her lips to mine.

And this time, she feels it too.

"You shouldn't touch me like that if you don't mean it," I manage, voice rougher than I intended.

She turns to face me, and I can see the confusion in her eyes. The way she's trying to understand what just happened.

"I didn't. The Ether did."

But then something shifts in her expression. Something that looks dangerously like decision.

"But maybe I won't stop it next time," she whispers.

Then she's walking away, leaving me standing in the corridor with silver mist still clinging to my skin like a promise.

I press my hand to my chest where the warmth lingers, where her magic sank into me like it belongs there.

"Not yours yet either," I whisper to the empty hallway.

But I hadn't moved when she touched me.

And worse—I didn't want to.

For the first time in centuries, I'm not sure who's hunting whom.

Chapter 42
BREE

Air. Now.

The garden hits me like a slap—cool and sharp against my flushed skin. But it doesn't help. Nothing's going to help the way my hands are still shaking from that moment in the hallway.

"You shouldn't touch me like that if you don't mean it."

Thanc's voice keeps echoing in my head, rough and raw and nothing like his usual controlled tone. The way his silver eyes went dark when I brushed past him, like I'd lit something on fire that he'd been trying to keep buried.

God, I'm such an idiot.

Because the worst part isn't that I didn't mean it. The worst part is that I absolutely did, and now I can't stop thinking about what would have happened if I hadn't walked away.

I don't even know who I am most days. How could I possibly know what I want? It can't be that simple—just touch someone and suddenly understand something fundamental about yourself. But standing there in that hallway, feeling his magic respond to mine...

For a second, it felt like the easiest thing in the world.

The Ether swirls around my feet as I walk, agitated silver mist that acts just how I'm feeling inside. I need space. Distance from the sanctuary's warm walls and the guys' careful attention and the weight of expectations I never asked for.

Something glints near the base of the old oak tree—metal catching what little moonlight filters through the leaves. I kneel and push aside a tangle of vines, fingers closing around something that makes my skin crawl the second I touch it.

A hand mirror.

The frame is tarnished silver, but not in a normal way. It's all twisted curves and spirals that flow up into sharp points like horns or antlers. The metal should be dirty after lying in the garden dirt, covered in rust or moss. Instead, it's pristine. Like someone just polished it and set it down five minutes ago.

I lift it to see it better in the moonlight, and my breath catches.

For just a moment—maybe three seconds—my eyes in the reflection glow deep red. Not reflecting light, but actually glowing from within like embers. The sight makes my stomach lurch, but I can't look away. Then they fade to black. Completely black. No iris, no pupil, just endless dark that seems to swallow light.

What the fuck?!

I jerk the mirror away from my face, heart hammering. When I force myself to look again, normal green eyes stare back at me. But everything else is still wrong. My reflection wavers like I'm looking at myself through water, edges blurring and shifting. Like there are two versions of me trying to occupy the same space and failing.

The mist swirls closer when I keep staring, silver tendrils reaching toward the mirror's surface with something that feels like curiosity. But cautious curiosity. Like it recognizes something I don't.

It's just a trick of the light, I tell myself. *Just some random piece of junk someone dropped.*

But I pocket it anyway, because leaving it feels wrong even though keeping it feels worse.

"You always wander off alone when the moon's this high?"

I spin toward the voice, heart hammering. Seth steps out from the tree line, hands visible and expression concerned rather than threatening. He keeps his distance, respecting the space between us.

"You startled me," I say, pressing a hand to my chest.

"Sorry. I saw you out here and thought you might need company." His voice is warm, actually apologetic. "Or backup, depending on what kind of night you're having."

I can't help but smile a little. "The kind where I need to walk off some really stupid decisions before I make even worse ones."

"Ah. One of those." Seth nods like he gets it completely. "Want to talk about it, or should I just walk quietly and be confused from a safe distance?"

There's something refreshing about how straightforward he is. No careful probing, no trying to read my emotions through magical intuition. Just a simple offer I can take or leave.

"People," I say finally. "Complicated people making everything way more complicated than it needs to be."

"Nobody tells you what happens when you get power you never asked for," Seth says quietly. "How suddenly everyone has opinions about what you should do with it. Who you should trust. How you should feel about everything."

He's right—everyone does have opinions. About my magic, my choices, whether I'm safe. Even when they mean well, it feels like drowning in other people's certainty about my life. But he gets it.

"Exactly." The word comes out like a breath I didn't know I was holding. "Sometimes I just want to make one normal decision without everyone analyzing it for hidden dangers."

Seth takes a step closer, slow and unthreatening. "Must be hard, learning to trust yourself when everyone else thinks they know better."

That's when I notice something weird. The mist that's been swirling around my feet since I left the house suddenly goes completely still. Not pulling away from Seth, not reaching toward him either. Just... stopping. Like it's holding its breath.

I glance down, puzzled by the sudden calm, but Seth's voice draws my attention back.

"What's that?" he asks, nodding at my pocket where the mirror's outline shows.

"Just some old mirror. Probably fell out of someone's stuff." I pull it out, turning the creepy frame over in my hands. Under the moonlight, those twisted horn-things look even worse. "Found it buried under the vines."

Seth stares at it way longer than seems normal. Something shifts in his expression—like he recognizes it.

"That's a dangerous thing to find in a place like this."

"It's just a mirror."

"Is it?" His voice goes oddly casual. Too casual. "Not everything that shows you a reflection tells you the truth. Some mirrors show you what you want to see. Others show you what someone else wants you to see."

The mist around my feet flickers, going dim like a candle in the wind.

Ice runs down my spine. There's something in the way he says it—like he knows exactly what this thing is and what it does.

"What do you mean by that?"

Seth glances toward the tree line for just a second—quick, like he's checking something. When he looks back, his expression is perfectly pleasant again.

"Just old stories. Places like this, they collect things. Not all of them friendly."

But before he can answer, the sanctuary door slams open with enough force to echo across the garden.

Theo bursts out, breathless and wild-eyed, scanning the darkness until his gaze locks onto us. Something passes across his face—relief, then recognition, then pure alarm.

He's running before I can call out to him, feet pounding across the gravel path.

"Get away from her!" he shouts, voice cracking with urgency.

I stumble backward, startled by the raw panic in his voice. Seth raises his hands, stepping back with calm surprise, but Theo doesn't slow down.

He reaches us in seconds, putting himself between me and Seth with protective fury written across every line of his body.

"Theo, what—"

"Don't," he says, not taking his eyes off Seth. "Something's wrong. I saw—" He swallows hard, chest heaving. "I had a vision. You're in danger."

My heart pounds against my ribs, adrenaline flooding my system as I look between them. Seth's expression is carefully neutral, confused but not angry. Theo's is desperate, certain, afraid.

And in my pocket, the mirror feels suddenly, impossibly heavy.

Like it's been waiting for this moment all along.

Chapter 43
THEO

The vision still burns behind my eyes as I burst through the sanctuary doors, breathless and wild-eyed, scanning the darkness until my gaze locks onto them. Something passes across my face—relief, then recognition, then pure alarm.

Seth. From the morning walks. The one Jace mentioned—said he'd been around Bree. Too much.

I'm running before anyone can call out to me, feet pounding across the gravel path.

"Get away from her!" I shout, voice cracking with urgency.

Bree stumbles backward, startled by the raw panic in my voice. Seth raises his hands, stepping back with calm surprise, but I don't slow down.

I reach them in seconds, shoving myself between Bree and Seth, muscles tight with fury I don't remember choosing.

"Theo, what—"

"Don't," I say, not taking my eyes off Seth. "Something's wrong. I saw—" I swallow hard, chest heaving. "I had a vision. You're in danger."

But Seth looks... completely normal. Just confused. Just Seth.

"Were you about to—" My voice cracks again as I try to make sense of what I'm seeing versus what I saw. "What were you talking about?"

Seth steps back further, hands still visible, expression genuinely puzzled. "We were just talking about the garden. She was showing me around."

For a second, the vision overlaps what I'm seeing—Seth's face flickering between solid and broken, real and reflected. I blink hard, and he's just Seth again.

"In my vision, you were standing over her," I say, words tumbling out. "The Ether was wrong—black, like oil on water. Everything was ruined."

"Theo." Bree's voice cuts through my spiral, alarmed now. "You're scaring me. What's going on?"

I stare at Seth, trying to find any trace of the otherness I witnessed. Same face, same voice, but there's no threat here. He looks human in every way that matters.

But what if the vision was wrong? What if I'm losing control of my gift?

"I don't know," I admit, feeling completely unmoored. "I don't know what I saw."

Bree's expression shifts from alarm to concern—for me, not about some imaginary threat. She steps closer, her hand finding my arm, not pulling me closer—just anchoring me.

"Theo..." she says, and I can hear the conflict in her voice. "I want to talk about this," she says, softer now. "Just... let me clear my head first. Please?"

She's not stepping away from me. She's just... standing still. Choosing calm. I want to follow—but I know I'd just drag the panic with me.

I nod slowly, backing toward the sanctuary. As I reach the doors, I catch her turning back to Seth.

"Sorry," she says quietly. "I don't know what that was."

I know she'll come find me. She always does. It's the waiting that's hard.

The main hall feels too bright after the garden's shadows. The others are already there, drawn by whatever energy I put off when the vision hit, or maybe just by the sound of me crashing through the sanctuary like something was chasing me.

Rhett moves toward me immediately. "What happened? You look—"

"Where's Bree?" Gray interrupts, scanning the space behind me.

"Still outside," I say, the words tasting bitter.

"With who?" Jace's voice carries an edge I rarely hear.

"Seth."

Thane's gaze flicks between me and the direction I came from, but there's something off about him—an edge to his usual control, like he's holding himself together with sheer will. Something unreadable crosses his face. Without a word, he turns and slips back toward the garden entrance.

"Theo," Rhett says carefully. "Talk to us. What happened?"

I make it to the stone circle in the center of the hall, pressing my palms against the cool stone. The contact usually grounds me, helps me sort through whatever I've seen. Tonight the Ether here feels charged wrong—static electricity crackling through my bones, setting my teeth on edge.

"A vision," I say, dropping into the center. "But different. It felt real in a way that defies everything I understand about my gift."

Which admittedly isn't much.

The sanctuary's warm silver hum surrounds me. Familiar. Comforting. But then something like mirror-glass slices through my thoughts—too sharp to belong here.

Bree's shadow splits—one half reaching toward me, the other toward something hidden.

A door opening into a sanctuary that looks like ours—but hollow. Like the shape of the sanctuary had been remembered rather than lived in.

Whispers echoing in my own voice: "She doesn't belong here—yet. It's not time. You saw it already."

I surface gasping, the fragments scattering like startled birds. But the certainty remains—something is bleeding through from a place it has no business being. What I saw had the same layout—familiar, but wrong—like the vision didn't know how to interpret the place and stitched something together from pieces it thought I could understand.

"The vision was of our garden," I say finally. "But not our garden. Everything was in the right place, but... off. Changed. And Seth was there, but fractured. Like someone had tried to glue broken pieces into the shape of him."

Wes lowers himself beside me without a word, grounding me with the steadiness I couldn't find on my own. "And Bree?"

"Hurt. Dying, maybe. The Ether around her was black as night, rippling in patterns that felt wrong."

"But outside just now," Gray says, "everything looked normal."

"That's what I don't understand." I run my hands through my hair, frustration bleeding through. "This vision felt more alive than anything I've felt before. But Seth looked... he looked exactly like himself. Human. Confused."

Silence settles over the group like a weight. I can see the calculation in their faces—whether to go after her, whether to trust my vision, whether to trust me.

"Visions can be warnings," Stellan murmurs. "Or fragments. Not certainties."

"Can the visions lie to him?" Jace asks, but there's no edge to it. Just consideration.

Stellan's expression shifts slightly. "It's rare, but it's not impossible."

I sit in the circle's quiet after they drift away to give me space, replaying every detail. The changed garden. The fractured figure. Whispers in my own voice. The way Bree's shadow fell in two directions, like she was being pulled between worlds that shouldn't touch.

I open my palm—and stop breathing.

A thread of reflective mist rests on my skin. Not silver like Bree's Ether—dark as polished obsidian, gleaming with inner light.

I blink. It's gone.

The cold spot it leaves behind doesn't fade. Like it touched me back.

What if the vision was a warning? What if a door's been opened and something's already walked through?

Chapter 44
THANE

I step into the garden through the sanctuary's side door, drawn by voices drifting through the night air. The hunger claws at me, but it's not the same hunger I've known for centuries. Three weeks. Three weeks since I last fed, since she opened that door and everything I understood about myself began to unravel.

Three weeks of telling myself I'm choosing not to feed. Of convincing myself it's strategy, control, protection of her.

But the truth I won't admit—can't admit—sits like ice in my chest: I've tried. Twice. Fed on willing donors in the camps when the need became unbearable.

And felt nothing. No satisfaction. No sustenance. Just emptiness that left me hungrier than before.

The scent hits me first. Vanilla and honey, undercut with something wilder that makes my fangs ache behind my lips. But there's another scent too. Male. Unfamiliar. Wrong.

I move silent as shadow between the mira trees, violet-purple leaves catching moonlight as I track the voices to their source.

"—really is beautiful here," Seth is saying, his tone warm, genuine.

"I think it responds to emotion," Bree replies, and I can hear the soft smile in her voice. "Maybe it picks up on whatever we're feeling."

I stop breathing. That's the voice she uses when she's unguarded. When she's not watching every word, calculating what might be safe to say.

I've watched her use it with the others over these past weeks—with Wes when he brings her tea, with Jace when he makes her laugh, with all of them. Everyone but Stellan and me.

She trusts him.

Something cold and vicious unfurls as I catch sight of them through the branches. Bree sitting on the stone bench, relaxed in ways she isn't around me. Seth beside her, close enough that their knees almost touch.

Close enough to hurt her before I could intervene.

The hunger sharpens, but not for blood. For more. For something that might not exist anymore.

What if I can't feed from anyone? The thought surfaces before I can bury it. *What if whatever she's done to me is permanent?*

What if I'm broken?

"I should probably head back," Seth says, rising from the bench. "Thank you for showing me around. For... everything."

"Anytime," Bree says, and the easy generosity in her voice makes something twist behind my ribs.

"Goodnight, Bree."

"Goodnight."

The simple exchange shouldn't feel like a knife to the chest. Shouldn't make every instinct I have roar with the need to eliminate a threat that might not even be there.

Seth walks away, disappearing into the shadows beyond the garden. But Bree doesn't follow. She stays on the bench, tilting her head back to look at the stars filtering through the mira leaves.

Then she reaches into her pocket and pulls something out. Something that catches the moonlight and throws it back in fractured silver.

A mirror.

My blood turns to ice. Small, handheld, but there's something wrong about it. The frame is all spirals and curves that flow into sharp points like horns. The surface seems to drink light rather than reflect it properly, and even from here I can sense something ancient and hungry about it.

She's holding it up, studying her reflection in the moonlight, completely unaware of what she might be looking into.

What might be looking back.

Pain flares beneath my ribs, sudden and searing.

The Council summons burns through my flesh like acid, and I barely bite back a curse as the magic wraps around me like chains. Not now. Not when she's alone in the garden, unprotected, trusting—

The magic tears me sideways through space before I can do anything but watch her sitting alone beneath the purple leaves.

The Chamber of Five materializes around me in a rush of cold stone and calculated malice. Same black throne, same position of deliberate inferiority. But this time, something's different.

The tension in the room is sharp enough to cut.

Valdris stands perfectly still, flames dying to embers at her feet. Marcus sits rigid in his steel throne, fingers steepled. Nyx lounges with predatory stillness that means someone's about to bleed.

And Eris—Eris is staring directly at me with silver eyes that see too much.

"You're late," Valdris says.

"I wasn't summoned. I was dragged."

"Semantics." Marcus's voice cuts like frost. "The result is the same."

"Three more surges," Eris says, her voice hollow and distant. "Stronger each time. The girl is not stabilizing. She's escalating."

Every muscle in my body goes tight. They're talking about Bree—of course they are. But this time it's not just observation or strategy. Her power is escalating beyond what they expected.

It's not something they can ignore any longer.

"She's learning control," I say, keeping my voice level even as something violent claws at my ribs.

"Control?" Nyx laughs, sharp and mocking. "Darling, half the magical community felt her last flare. She's not controlling anything—she's broadcasting."

"The situation is contained—"

"The situation," Valdris interrupts, "is that an untrained Source is gathering followers and power in equal measure. You were sent to assess her, not court her."

The words cut deep. I force myself not to react, but something cold settles in my stomach.

"I've been monitoring—"

"You've been compromised." Marcus's tone is flat, final. "It was expected. Feeders are notoriously susceptible to Source influence."

Susceptible. Like what I feel for her is weakness. Like the way my entire existence has shifted around her presence is just magical compulsion.

But there's something else in his tone. Something that cuts deeper.

"Perhaps," Nyx adds with that razor-sharp smile of hers, "it's not her Ether that compromised you. Perhaps your appetite is simply... failing."

The words hit like ice water in my veins. Because she's not wrong.

Because I haven't been able to feed properly since I met Bree. Because every attempt leaves me emptier than before. Because what used to sustain me for centuries now tastes like ash and desperation.

The hunger twists, becomes something desperate and frightening.

"Seventy-two hours," Valdris says. "Bring her to the neutral ground at Thornfield. Alive, unharmed, and willing to submit to Council judgment."

"And if she refuses?"

"She won't," Eris says softly. "Not if you explain the alternative."

Something in her tone makes my blood run cold. "What alternative?"

Marcus smiles—thin and sharp as a blade. "If you fail to retrieve her, we're sending a replacement. Someone less... entangled."

The words ring like a death knell in my ears. Because I know exactly what kind of replacement they'd send. What kind of operative has no qualms about breaking an untrained Source into compliance.

"Who?"

"Phil Donnahue," Valdris says. "He's been monitoring her for the past ten years, most recently posing as her landlord. He volunteered. Quite enthusiastically, actually."

My stomach drops. Phil. I know the name from reports, but this is the first I'm hearing about a decade-long operation. The hybrid who's been in her life all this time—shifter instincts wrapped in mentalist precision. Close enough to hunt her scent, her Ether trails, and break her mind piece by piece whenever the Council gave the word.

"You can't." The words tear out of me before I can stop them. "He'll destroy her."

"He'll do what you apparently cannot." Marcus leans forward. "He'll bring her home."

"This *is* her home!"

Silence. Four sets of eyes watching me with varying degrees of satisfaction. Like they've been waiting for me to crack.

"Attachment," Nyx purrs. "How... predictable."

The hunger roars to life, making my fangs extend fully. Making every careful mask I wear crack at the edges.

"After that, Phil has lethal authority if she resists."

The Council's magic tears me away from the chamber, depositing me back in the sanctuary garden like discarded refuse. Everything feels different now. Sharper. More urgent.

She's still here. Safe—for now. But for how long?

The hunger claws at me, made worse by the Council's casual dismissal of what I feel for her. *Susceptible.* Like centuries of survival mean nothing against Source influence.

Maybe they're right. Maybe that's all this is.

But it doesn't feel like compulsion when I think about her trusting Seth. When I remember the way she said goodnight to him, easy and unguarded.

It feels like something far more dangerous.

Every instinct I have is screaming. The need to make sure she's safe. To eliminate every threat before they can touch her.

But underneath it all, a more terrifying realization crystallizes.

I can't go back to strangers and shadows. To surviving on casual violence and detached hunger. That version of me died the moment she looked at me like I mattered.

Whatever she's done to me—whatever I've become because of her—there's no undoing it.

Chapter 45
BREE

The mirror feels cold in my hands as I turn it over, watching moonlight catch the surface and disappear. Not reflect—disappear. Like the light falls into it and never comes back out.

Seth's footsteps faded into the shadows, but I'm still sitting here. Still thinking about Theo crashing through those doors like something was chasing him. The raw panic in his voice when he yelled at Seth.

Get away from her.

Like Seth was a threat. Like I was in danger.

But Seth had looked as confused as I felt. Just a man showing concern when someone started yelling. Concern for me like I mattered.

So why does my chest feel tight when I think about it?

I trace the mirror's twisted frame with my thumb. The way my reflection wavered in it earlier, the way my eyes glowed red then went completely black... it should terrify me.

Instead, it just feels important. Like something I was meant to find.

I'm not scared of it, I tell myself. *But maybe I should be.*

I feel him before I hear him, like a shiver down my spine I'm not sure if I'm ready for or not.

"You're always watching," I say to the darkness behind me.

His voice comes low and controlled: "You shouldn't have been out here alone."

"You weren't here to stop me."

Silence. When I glance back, he looks wrecked. Not his usual composed mask, but something raw and barely held together. His silver eyes are too bright, his jaw set like he's grinding his teeth.

"Why are you really here?" I ask, turning to face him fully.

He doesn't answer immediately. Just moves closer, his gaze flicking to the mirror in my hands, then to my face. Something dangerous flickers behind his careful control.

"Where did you get that?"

"The garden. I found it earlier buried under the vines by the oak tree." I hold it up between us. "Do you know what it is?"

His expression goes carefully blank. "You shouldn't be touching it."

"That's not an answer."

"It's the only answer you're getting."

I stand, frustration flaring. "I'm tired of people deciding what I can and can't handle. First Theo with his panic attack, now you with your cryptic warnings—"

"Theo was right to panic."

The words cut through my anger like ice water. I stare at him, processing the absolute certainty in his voice.

"What do you mean?"

Instead of answering, he steps closer. His hand lifts, hovering near my face like he wants to touch me but doesn't quite dare.

"You have no idea what you're dealing with," he says quietly. "What any of this means."

"Then tell me."

His fingers brush my cheek, just barely. The contact sends heat shooting down my spine, but there's something desperate in the way he touches me. Like he's trying to memorize the feeling.

I don't flinch. I should—contact like this usually makes my body freeze or pull away—but I don't. When did that change? When did I start feeling safe enough with him, with anyone, that my body doesn't brace for impact?

"I can't."

"Can't or won't?"

His thumb traces along my jawline, and I feel his control crack just slightly. "Both."

That's when his hand slips lower, fingers grazing the cluster of scars along my collarbone where my shirt has shifted. For a second, I'm amazed by how it feels—gentle, reverent, like he's touching something precious instead of damaged. The moment his skin makes contact—

The world explodes.

Not light. Memory.

I'm twelve years old, hiding in my bedroom closet. My father's voice drifts up the stairs, sickly sweet and patient.

"Bree, sweetheart, where are you? Daddy just wants to talk."

I press deeper into the closet, knowing he'll find me eventually. Knowing what happens when he stops using that fake-gentle voice.

I gasp, jerking backward, but the memory clings like smoke. Thane staggers, his hand falling away from my skin like I've burned him.

"What the hell did you just do?" My voice comes out shaky, raw.

He looks as shattered as I feel, silver eyes wide with something like horror. "I didn't—I don't know how—"

"You saw it." It's not a question. I can see the knowledge written across his face, the way he's looking at me like I'm broken glass. "You felt what I felt."

He nods once, sharp and pained.

"That was the first time I realized no one was coming to stop him," I whisper.

"You were just a child."

"So were you, once."

Something shifts in his expression. Raw recognition, maybe. Or grief. He reaches for me again, instinctively, his hand slipping lower to graze the cluster of scars along my collarbone where my shirt has shifted. For a second, I'm amazed by how it feels—gentle, reverent, like he's touching something precious instead of damaged. The moment our skin connects—

Another flash.

Suddenly my body is larger, stronger, built like a predator. The room dim around me as I look into the eyes of a young man.

"Yes, just this once."

I don't hesitate, my fangs extending, sinking into his willing flesh. He moans beneath me, body arching into the bite, lost in his own pleasure. But the hunger claws at me, desperate and aching, while I close my eyes and pretend it's her skin beneath my lips. Her pulse, her warmth, her choice. But it's not. His blood tastes like ash as it coats my tongue. It's not her. Not what I really want, not who I need. And somehow the hunger is worse than before I started. We break apart, both breathing hard.

Suddenly I'm back in my own body, smaller, softer, but still shaking from the memory of being him. Of feeling his desperation, his hunger, his shame.

Thane looks wrecked. Not just shattered like before—mortified. Like I've seen something he never meant for anyone to know.

"Is that what it's like when you feed?" I ask quietly.

"Not like that." His voice is barely a whisper. "Not ever. Not until you."

The space between us feels charged, electric. I take a step closer, drawn by something I don't entirely understand.

"What if I want to be different?"

The words hang between us. Something shifts in his expression—hunger, maybe, or need. His careful control cracks just a little.

"Bree—"

"I'm not a child anymore," I say softly. "And I'm not afraid of you."

He moves then, suddenly, backing me toward the low stone wall that separates the garden from the world beyond. Not aggressive—urgent. Like he can't help himself anymore.

My back meets stone. His hands brace on either side of me, caging me in but not trapping me. I could slip away if I wanted.

I don't want to.

"Tell me to stop," he breathes against my ear.

"No."

Chapter 46
THANE

"Tell me to stop," I breathe against her ear.

"No."

The single word breaks something in me. Not my control—that's been fracturing since the moment she touched me. Something deeper. Something I thought I'd buried centuries ago.

Hope.

I pull back just enough to see her face in the moonlight. Her green eyes are steady, certain, and there's no fear in them. There should be. After everything she's seen, everything I've shown her—the hunger, the desperation, the way I've fed on others while thinking of her—there should be wariness. Calculation. Self-preservation.

Instead, there's trust.

"Bree." Her name feels sacred on my tongue. "Are you sure?"

She nods, her hands finding the buttons of my shirt. Her fingers tremble slightly, but not with fear. With something that makes the air between us hum with possibility.

"I've seen inside you," she whispers, working the first button free. "The shame, the hunger, all of it. And I'm still here."

The cotton falls open under her touch, and she places her palm flat against my chest. The warmth of her skin burns through me like salvation.

"You saw me too," she continues, voice barely audible. "In that closet. How small I felt. How hopeless. And you didn't flinch."

"Never." The word comes out rough, absolute. "You could show me every scar, every fear, every broken piece, and I would never flinch."

She tilts her head back, studying my face. "Then show me."

I cup her face in my hands, thumbs brushing over her cheekbones. She leans into the touch like it's something she's been craving, and the simple gesture undoes me completely.

When I kiss her, it's not with the hunger that's been clawing at me for weeks. It's reverent. Worshipful. Like I'm finally touching something sacred after centuries of emptiness.

She melts against me, her body soft and warm and willing. The Ether around her ankles responds, silver mist curling up to wrap around us both like approval. Like blessing.

I've never made love to someone. Fed from them, yes. Used them for sustenance, for momentary relief from the endless hunger. But this—touching her not because I need to take something, but because I want to give everything I have—this is new.

Her shirt hits the ground first, then mine. She doesn't hide from me, doesn't cover the faint scars that map her history across pale skin. Instead, she watches my face as I trace them with gentle fingers, learning each mark like scripture.

"Beautiful," I whisper, because it's the only word that fits. Not despite the scars, but including them. All of her.

She shivers under my touch, but presses closer. "Your turn," she murmurs, hands exploring the planes of my chest, the old wounds that mark my own history. Her fingers are soft, curious, mapping me like she wants to memorize every inch.

I cup her face, thumb brushing over her bottom lip. When she parts her lips and presses a kiss to my thumb, the simple gesture nearly undoes me.

"Bree," I breathe, and she answers by pulling me down to her mouth.

The kiss is slow, deep, tasting of trust and desire. Her hands tangle in my hair, holding me to her like she's afraid I might disappear. But I'm not going anywhere. Not now. Not ever, if she'll have me.

My hands shake as I work at the fastenings of her remaining clothes, her helping, both of us urgent now but still careful. Still reverent. When skin finally meets skin completely, we both go still for a heartbeat, overwhelmed by the sensation.

When I lift her onto the stone wall, she wraps her legs around my waist and pulls me closer, her breath warm against my throat. The rough stone presses against her back, but she doesn't seem to care. All her attention is on me, on us, on this moment.

"I choose this," she says against my ear, voice barely a whisper. "I choose you."

The words hit me like lightning. Not just permission—choice. Active, deliberate selection of me, of this moment, of whatever comes after.

"Are you certain?" I ask one more time, because I need to be sure. Need to know this is what she wants.

Her answer is to guide me to her. I gasp her name as I press inside her slowly, carefully. The feeling of being joined with her—body and soul—is indescribable. Like finding something I didn't even know I'd lost.

"Thane." My name on her lips sounds like prayer, like benediction, like home.

I move slowly at first, watching her face in the moonlight, learning what makes her breath catch, what makes her arch against me. She's responsive, open, meeting each movement with her own. Her hands clutch at my shoulders, nails digging in just enough to ground us both.

She arches again, breath catching. "I didn't know it could feel like this," she whispers.

And fuck if that doesn't ruin me.

"More," she says softly.

Who am I to deny her anything?

The rhythm builds between us, natural as breathing. The Ether swirls around us, growing brighter with each movement, each soft sound she makes. It doesn't feel like magic responding to emotion—it feels like recognition. Like coming home.

I lose myself in her warmth, her scent, the way she says my name when I hit that perfect spot inside her. For the first time in centuries, the hunger quiets. Not because I'm feeding, but because I'm being fed. Being chosen. Being seen as more than just a weapon or a monster.

She's close—I can feel it in the way she trembles, the way her breath comes in short gasps against my ear. I reach between us, finding the spot that makes her arch and cry out.

"Let go," I whisper against her lips. "I've got you."

"I don't know if I can," she breathes, vulnerable and trusting all at once.

"Anything you need," I murmur, meaning it completely. "Whatever you need."

I shift the angle, the pressure, watching her face until I find what breaks her open. She shatters around me with a sound that's half-sob, half-prayer, my name falling from her lips again and again. Her body clenches around mine, waves of pleasure pulling me deeper.

The sight of her, lost in ecstasy and glowing with power, pushes me over the edge. I follow her into release with a groan that comes from somewhere deep in my chest, somewhere that's been empty for too long.

But as the pleasure peaks, as I pour myself into her, the hunger stirs. Not the cold, calculating need I've carried for centuries—something warmer. Deeper. A craving for connection that goes beyond blood.

My fangs extend without my permission.

"Bree," I gasp, trying to pull back. "I can't—I don't want to hurt—"

She tangles her fingers in my hair and tilts her head, exposing the long line of her throat. "Now," she breathes. "Please."

The trust in those two words breaks me.

I strike swift and clean, fangs sinking into the soft skin just below her pulse point just as the last waves of climax wash through us both. Her blood hits my tongue like liquid starlight—warm and bright and tasting of power, of choice, of gift freely given.

She cries out, her body arching against mine as the bite sends another wave of pleasure crashing through her. I feel her clench around me again, her nails digging into my shoulders as the sensation overwhelms her. The feeding doesn't just nourish me—it ignites her, sends her spiraling into a second peak that leaves her trembling and breathless in my arms.

The connection that blooms between us is unlike anything I've ever experienced. Not just her blood feeding my hunger, but something more. A tethering of souls that goes both ways. I feel her pleasure mixing with mine, her trust wrapping around my heart like armor.

And then I feel it lock into place.

The bond that began weeks ago in the attic—when her Ether first curled around my boots, reaching for something it somehow recognized—finally completes itself. The Ether doesn't just respond to the bite with silver light. It shifts and becomes something richer. Not just her power—our power. Connected. Chosen.

Somewhere beneath her skin, I sense rather than see a scar warming. Glowing. The physical mark of what we've just sealed.

She doesn't notice. But I do.

I withdraw my fangs carefully, sealing the small wounds with my tongue. The taste of her lingers, sweet and perfect and mine.

We stay joined as the intensity fades, my forehead now pressed against hers, both of us breathing hard.

"I didn't mean for that to happen," I whisper, because it's true. I'd planned to wait. To prove I could choose restraint over hunger.

She laughs softly, the sound vibrating through both our chests. "Yes, you did. And so did I."

Her fingers trace the line of my jaw, gentle and sure. "I felt what you felt. The hunger wasn't just for blood, was it?"

I close my eyes, overwhelmed by how completely she sees me. "No. It was for this. For connection. For someone to choose me not because they had to, but because they wanted to."

"Then you have it." She tilts my chin up until I meet her gaze. "You have me."

The words settle into my chest like warmth, like home, like everything I never dared to hope for. I kiss her again, soft and grateful and full of promises I'm not sure I know how to keep but desperately want to try.

We're quiet for a long moment, just holding each other as the garden settles around us. The Ether has calmed to a gentle silver glow that pools around our feet like moonlight. Everything feels possible. Perfect.

That's when I hear it.

A voice, distant but carrying on the night air. Too far for her to catch with human hearing, but clear as day to me.

Seth.

"Tell Phil she's found the mirror."

The words hit me like ice water. My entire body goes rigid, and I have to fight not to react visibly. Bree is still soft in my arms, still glowing with contentment and trust. She doesn't know.

She can't know. Not yet.

I force my breathing to stay steady, my arms to remain gentle around her. But inside, everything has shifted. The warmth from moments before turns cold and sharp.

Seth. The friend she trusts. The man she's been confiding in, showing around the sanctuary, treating like family.

He's been reporting to Phil.

The betrayal cuts deeper than any physical wound ever could. Not just the betrayal of her trust, but the timing. Right now, while I'm still inside her, while the taste of her blood is still on my tongue, while the bond between us is new and precious and fragile—someone she trusts is selling her out.

I press my face against her neck, breathing in her scent, committing this moment to memory. Because everything is about to change. Again.

And this time, I won't let her face it alone.

"We should go inside," I murmur against her ear, keeping my voice steady through sheer force of will. "It's getting cold."

She nods sleepily, trusting and content. As I help her down from the wall, as I gather our scattered clothes, as I lead her back toward the sanctuary's warm lights, I'm already planning.

Seth made one critical mistake.

He assumed no one was listening.

But I heard every word. And now I know exactly what we're up against.

The game has changed.

And Bree doesn't even know it yet.

THANK YOU

To my readers: You are the magic that makes this all possible. Thank you for following Bree deeper into the mist, for falling in love with her chosen family, and for trusting me with your hearts as this story unfolds. Your enthusiasm, your reviews, your messages telling me how these characters have touched your lives—that's what keeps me writing.

Thank you for seeing yourselves in Bree's journey of healing. For cheering when she finds her strength. For understanding that love doesn't always look like fairy tales, but it's real and powerful and worth fighting for.

Thank you for being patient as Bree learns to trust, as the boys discover their powers, and as everyone figures out that sometimes the best families are the ones we choose.

To anyone who has ever felt broken or unworthy of love: Bree's story is for you. You are not too damaged to be loved. You are not too much or too little. You deserve all the good things, including people who see your worth even when you can't see it yourself.

To everyone who believes in second chances, found family, and the magic of letting yourself be truly seen: This one's for you.

Here's to stepping into the unknown, trusting the people who choose to walk beside us, and discovering that sometimes the most powerful magic is simply allowing ourselves to be loved.

SNEAK PEEK: ASHEN OATH

Sneak Peek: Ashen Oath

BREE

Sleep isn't happening.

I've tried every position, counted sheep, even attempted some deep breathing thing Theo taught me once. Nothing works. Every time I close my eyes, my brain cycles through everything—what happened with Thane in the garden, Theo's panicked vision, the way he looked so shaken. And poor Seth caught in the middle of it all.

I should have found Theo when I came back inside. Should have made sure he was okay. But by the time Thane and I... by the time we came back from the garden, he was nowhere to be found, and asking the others felt like admitting I'd failed him somehow.

So now I'm lying here replaying the way Thane's hands felt on my skin. The way he said my name when his fangs found my throat. The way the bond snapped into place between us, silver and warm and permanent.

Like forever. That kind of permanent.

And the way I walked away from Theo when he needed me, because apparently I'm excellent at letting people down.

What are the others going to think? The thought hits me like ice water. I spent years pushing them all away, convincing myself it was safer for everyone if I kept my distance. Then I finally let them close, and the first thing I do is... this. With Thane. With someone who was supposed to be watching me for the Council.

Did I just screw up everything we were building here? Everything I thought we were building?

My chest tightens. Will they think I chose him over them? Will they decide this is too complicated, too messy, too much? Maybe this will be the thing that finally makes them walk away.

I press my palms against my eyes, trying to stop the spiral. But the fear sits there, cold and familiar.

You don't have to be whole to be worthy of being seen.

Theo's words from the living room float back to me. When everything had just fallen apart and I thought I'd lost them all. When he looked at me like I mattered, broken pieces and all.

I have to believe they'll stick around no matter who I end up with. I have to believe that what we've built together is stronger than my fears.

Even if I'm not sure I believe it yet.

I roll over for the hundredth time, burying my face in pillows that smell like lavender and starlight. The sanctuary bedroom should feel like peace—with its curved walls and silver script that pulses gently in the moonlight streaming through the dome above. Everything here was built for comfort.

Instead, I feel like I'm vibrating out of my skin.

That's when I notice it.

The mirror from the garden sits on the bedside table where I left it before crawling into bed. The same twisted silver frame with spirals and curves that flow into sharp points like horns or antlers. The surface that drinks light instead of reflecting it properly, ancient and hungry.

I should leave it alone. After what I saw earlier—my eyes glowing red, then going completely black. Both Seth and Thane seemed uneasy about it too. I should probably throw the damn thing out a window.

Instead, I reach for it.

The metal is warm under my fingers, and I can't tell if that's from my own body heat or something else entirely. Something that makes my pulse quicken.

My reflection stares back, all messy hair and wide eyes. Pretty standard post-crisis look for me. But as I tilt it to catch the moonlight, something shifts.

The surface ripples.

I blink hard, wondering if I'm finally losing it. But when I look again, I'm not seeing myself anymore.

I'm seeing the corridor from earlier.

The scene plays out in perfect detail, but from an angle I never had. I watch myself move toward Thane, silver mist trailing behind me like a living thing. But there are details I missed—the way the Ether reaches for him before I'm even close, wrapping around his boots like it's claiming territory.

And his face when he thinks I'm not looking. Less controlled. More raw.

Like he's seeing something he wants and dreads in equal measure.

My heart does something complicated as I watch the scene unfold. When mirror-me brushes past him, I swear I feel the ghost of that contact. But it's what happens next that makes me sit up straighter.

A thread of silver light passes between us where the Ether touched him. Just for a heartbeat—a connection that glows like captured starlight.

I didn't see that. Couldn't have seen it.

"What the hell?" I whisper.

The image ripples again, and suddenly I'm looking at Thane alone in ruins. Cracked stone walls, pale light filtering through broken spaces. He's kneeling before what looks like a scrying mirror, and silver mist is rising from its shattered edges—my Ether, somehow reaching across distance.

He's pressing his hand to his chest, right over his heart, and his expression is completely unguarded. Stunned. Like his entire world just shifted and he doesn't know which way is up anymore.

Like he's just realized I've been here all along.

The scene fades, leaving me staring at my own reflection again. But now I look different—pupils dilated, breathing shallow. Like I've just seen something I wasn't supposed to.

I set the mirror down, my hands not quite steady. "Okay. Either I'm having a breakdown, or you're showing me things that actually happened."

The sigils around the frame pulse once, faint but deliberate.

"Great. Of course you are."

Against every instinct I have, I pick it up again. Because apparently I never learn.

This time, when the surface ripples, I'm looking at the sanctuary again. But wrong.

The main hall stretches out before me, its familiar curved walls and silver script. Except something's off. The script still glows, but it feels hollow somehow, like an echo of warmth rather than warmth itself. And I'm there, but not me. This version stands frozen in the center while the boys reach for her with desperate hands.

Rhett, Jace, Gray, Theo, Wes, Thane—and others behind them, faces I can almost recognize—but their faces are twisted with something between hunger and panic. And she's backing away from them, the Ether around her feet gone black as spilled ink.

Behind them all, barely visible in the shadows, stands someone I don't recognize. Tall, watching, with an intensity that makes my skin prickle.

The other-me opens her mouth like she's trying to speak, but no sound comes through the glass. The black Ether spreads outward from her feet, and everyone it touches—

I jerk the mirror away from my face, heart hammering against my ribs.

"Okay, that's enough of that."

I set it down more carefully this time, but I can't stop staring at it. The frame glows faintly in the moonlight, keeping time with my pulse.

Outside, footsteps echo in the corridor—someone doing a final check before bed. The normalcy of it should be comforting. Instead, it makes me think of that other version of myself, reaching for something I couldn't quite see.

I grab the blanket and pull it over my head like that'll help. But even with my eyes closed, I can feel the mirror's presence. Waiting. Watching.

Just another glamorous night in paradise, I think, borrowing my own sarcasm for comfort.

But it doesn't help. My heart won't stop racing, and every time I close my eyes, I see that other version of myself with the black Ether spreading around her feet. Not evil—just different. Wrong in a way I can't name.

A faint scent drifts through the room—chamomile and something sweeter, like honey and vanilla. I sit up, frowning, and find a steaming mug on the nightstand beside the mirror.

It wasn't there before. I'm sure of it.

The sanctuary, I realize. Paying attention to what I need before I know I need it, just like always.

I reach for the mug, careful not to touch the mirror, and wrap my hands around the warm ceramic. The tea tastes like comfort and safety, like being held when the world gets too sharp around the edges. Just how Wes usually makes it—sweet, careful, like he knows what I need before I do.

My pulse slows. The terror in my chest eases to something manageable.

"Thank you," I whisper to the room, and the silver script on the walls pulses once, gentle as a heartbeat.

I finish the tea and set the mug back down. The calm should carry me straight into sleep.

It doesn't.

My brain keeps circling back to what I saw. That silver thread between Thane and me. The other sanctuary that felt hollow. My mirror-self with black Ether pooling around her feet.

I shift under the blankets, listening to the quiet. The tea helped, but didn't erase everything. I'm tired but not settled, balanced on that knife's edge where sleep might happen if I stop thinking.

Good luck with that.

A soft knock interrupts the silence. Deliberate, but not urgent. Not hesitant either.

I freeze. Maybe it's Theo, still shaken from his vision. Or Wes, drawn by whatever restless energy he's been carrying lately. But something about the rhythm feels different.

The door opens just enough for someone to slip through.

Stellan.

He stands in the doorway like he's waiting for permission to exist in the same space as me. Moonlight catches the sharp line of his jaw, but I can't read his expression from here.

He doesn't move closer. Doesn't speak. Just... waits.

There's a question in his stillness that I don't entirely understand. But somehow, I know what he's asking.

I tilt my head at him.

He crosses the room like he's done this before, but careful. No assumptions. When he reaches the bed, he pauses again.

"Okay?" he asks, voice barely above a whisper.

I nod.

He climbs onto the bed with that fluid grace of his, settling behind me without crowding. When his arm slides around my waist, I stiffen—because that's what I do—but he just murmurs, "Shh," once, low and calm.

His hold is loose. Present, but not possessive.

The knot in my chest starts to loosen. My breathing shifts to match his without me deciding to. The sharp edges that the tea couldn't quite reach begin to blur.

"How?" I whisper.

He's quiet for so long I think he won't answer. When he finally speaks, his voice is soft against my hair.

"Your peace matters more than what it costs me."

I should probably ask what he means. Should wonder what this is costing him.

Instead, I let myself sink back against him.

Whatever his magic is doing, it's working. The anxious spiral in my head slows, then stops. My eyelids get heavy in a way that feels natural instead of forced.

The visions from the mirror fade to background noise—still there, but manageable. Like turning down the volume on a song that was too loud.

The last thing I'm aware of is his steady breathing and the way his presence makes the room feel safer. Just as I'm drifting off, his arm tightens around me—barely, but enough that I feel it. Like he's anchoring me to something solid.

The last conscious thought I have is still wondering if that dark vision was a warning or a promise.

But at least now I'm not wondering alone.

About the Author

Zora Stone writes romantasy with teeth: fierce heroines, protective men who'd burn the world for them, and enough emotional wreckage to keep things interesting. When she's not plotting betrayals or steamy chaos, she's drinking iced coffee, dodging laundry, or daydreaming about enchanted forests.

You can find her online at:

Website: ZoraStone.com

TikTok | Instagram: @ZoraStoneAuthor

And on Amazon and Goodreads.

Want behind-the-scenes chaos and sneak peeks? ZoraStone.com/Influencers

ALSO BY ZORA STONE

The Ether Chronicles

Crown of the Mist

Into the Ether

Ashen Oath

Veil of Echoes

Shattering the Void

To the Final End

Arcanum Academy

Shadows of Change

Shadows Rising

Shadows Found

Shadows Revealed

www.ingramcontent.com/pod-product-compliance
Lightning Source LLC
Chambersburg PA
CBHW020055310726

48970CB00002B/330